AMISH FAMILY SECRETS

BOOK 5 THE AMISH BONNET SISTERS SERIES

SAMANTHA PRICE

CHAPTER 1

UNDER THE CLEAR sky with a spring breeze blowing Florence's dress, she stood outside Carter's house and stared into his eyes. She'd just agreed to marry Carter Braithwaite and leave the Amish community and her family behind, without knowing how it would work out for everyone. Could her family function without her, and how would her stepmother react once she found out Carter's real identity?

"We'll have to get you an apple orchard."

She laughed, loving Carter's thoughtfulness. "I don't think you can get one just like that."

"With money, you can do anything, trust me." A slight frown settled on his forehead. "Your orchard's not something you can pick up and take with you."

"I'll work something out with Wilma. It's technically mine, even though I've never had to say it."

"I hope you don't think your family will let you have

it just like that. You're leaving them and they won't be happy about it. Your decision will have ramifications and they won't all be pretty."

She knew part of that was true. "No one else can run the orchard and no one's interested in it, not really."

"When we're married, things will change."

"Can't we stay here? Live here in your cottage – after we get married, of course." She looked back at the orchard that her father had so lovingly tended over the years. The orchard that had grown along with her to become what it was today, one of the largest-producing organic orchards in the region.

"We can live wherever you want."

"I love it here and it's close to my orchard. My brothers aren't interested, so it would go to me."

"We don't need to talk about that now. It's a minor detail."

He was right about one thing. They didn't need to talk about it now. She didn't want to overpower him right away with her stubbornness. Better he find out about her bad points after they were married. She smiled to herself at the thought.

She had said she'd leave the community for him and that was what she intended to do, but it was the practicalities of doing so that weighed on her heavily. It hadn't been right to keep going backward and forward – *should she, or shouldn't she?* – and driving herself and Carter crazy.

"Where should we start?" he asked.

"I think we should start now, by you meeting Wilma. Too much has been kept in the dark, but thanks to Ezekiel who told them all I was flirting with you, they already know there's been something happening between us."

He swallowed hard. "You mean we should go see Wilma right now?"

"Yes, before either of us change your mind." She giggled when she realized what she'd just said.

He laughed too. "I won't be the one changing my mind. I've always been the consistent one in the relationship. I'm pleased you're finally catching up." He smiled at her. "It's just that I've gone this long with keeping everything quiet, and I don't know if I'm ready to meet her. If she was nothing to me apart from your stepmother, I wouldn't have this problem, but ..."

"You just asked me to marry you."

"I did and I'm ready for that. More than ready. I just don't know if I feel the same about meeting Wilma just yet."

"For our relationship to move ahead, we have to tell Wilma and everybody else the truth. I'm going to have to leave my community, so it's all going to be out in the open shortly."

"I'm sorry, I wish it didn't have to be that way. I don't want you to leave your community if you want to stay, but I guess that's the way it has to be."

She stared at him. It didn't have to be that way if he

3

would join them, but she knew that wasn't going to happen. He looked down at the ground. "I'm just scared she'll have a bad reaction to me."

It was odd for a big man like him to admit to his feelings. Amish men wouldn't have said anything like that. Wilma had been unpredictable of late and Florence searched for words of reassurance.

He sighed. "Tell me about your family before I meet them. Let's sit inside where it's warm and then I'll go back with you and … meet them."

"Okay."

Once they were seated together on the couch, he clasped both of her hands. "Tell me about your family. Start with your sisters – the bonnet sisters."

She giggled. "Oh no. You have to stop calling them that."

He chuckled. "I'll try, but I've been doing it for so long, it'll be hard. I can tell it upsets you from the little twitches on the side of your mouth when you're annoyed."

"You can?" That was something she didn't even know about herself.

He nodded.

"Well, you've met Honor. You helped me fetch her when she ran away."

"I won't ever forget that long drive."

Florence nodded. "I know. Mercy is the eldest, she's married and … well, both Mercy and Honor moved away and are living in a community in Connecticut.

They married brothers. I'm not too keen on Jonathon, Honor's husband."

"Yes, I know. I met him."

"That's right. I forgot. Oh, and Mercy just told us she's pregnant."

"Congratulations. You'll be an aunt."

"Half-aunt. As I'm so often reminded." When she saw him frowning, she shrugged off her annoyance at always being told she was a *half*-sister, and Wilma's *step*-daughter. "Sorry. I guess you can tell that bothers me."

"Got it. That's the oldest ones done with, and then we have … who?"

"Third oldest is Joy. We've become close since the older two have gone. She's gotten engaged to Isaac who's my older brother's wife's brother."

He trembled. "Wait. I have to think about that for a moment."

"I know. Most of our community members are related in some way through marriage, it seems. Everyone seems to be a second or third cousin to someone, too." She didn't wait for him to work it out. "The younger three are Hope, Favor, and then Cherish. Cherish is living away at the moment with Aunt Dagmar."

"You mentioned you have brothers?"

She nodded. "Two older brothers – full brothers. One owns a saddlery store in town and the other moved away just after our father died."

He nodded. "I think I'm getting the picture. Tell me about Wilma, your stepmother."

"Ah, well, she and I are very close … most of the time, except when she's reminding me I'm a *step* child. She has a best friend, Ada, and Ada's not happy with me at the moment."

He smirked. "What did you do?"

"She's the one who tried to match me with Ezekiel. Ezekiel was her idea."

"I see. And, if I hadn't been here, would you have succumbed to Ezekiel's charms?"

She giggled. Ezekiel didn't have any charms, but she couldn't be so rude as to say that. Ezekiel had tried, but not hard enough. He'd only come back into her life after he'd heard the rumors that she liked someone else. "I don't think so."

"You're not sounding very sure about that."

Looking into his eyes, she couldn't lie to him. "I do want children, Carter. If he could've offered me a good life where I could still work the orchard and raise children, maybe I would've married him. We got along okay."

"I hope you and I will get along better than okay."

She nodded. "We already do, from my side."

"I hope so. What we have is the real deal. I just know it. I'll do whatever makes you happy, Florence. I'll buy a dozen orchards, or we can build one together."

She laughed at his terminology. "Or even grow one."

"That too."

"Tell me, who are the people you're close to?"

He shrugged his shoulders. "I don't have anyone."

"Friends? Come on, you must have some friends. You've often said you don't have any, but you must have some."

"I've never had time for them. I've got people who work for me, but that's it."

She saw the sadness in his eyes.

"The thing I want more than anything is a family. I would love for us to have children, Florence."

"And I'd like nothing more."

"Will Wilma reject me after she hears about the connection between us?"

"I can't see that happening. She's been so upset for all these years for turning away Iris, your mother, that I think she'll be thrilled to see you."

"Does she know my mother has passed?"

"No, she wouldn't have any idea about that."

"I don't want to be the one to tell her. I don't want to be the one to turn up on the doorstep and tell her that her sister is dead. But you're right, we have to make a start somewhere. What do you intend to tell her? Do you want … are you going to tell her about us yet?"

Florence bit her lip thinking of the upheaval that

their news would cause. "I think that needs to be done slowly. We'll tell her about you, and let her think about that for a while. Then, maybe the other news – about us, I mean – might not be such a shock." She knew the community would turn their backs on her, but she hoped her family wouldn't. Some Amish families remained in contact with those who'd left. With her family by her side, she could still work the apple orchard, and that was one of the most important things to her.

He tugged on the neck of his T-shirt. "Do I look alright?"

She couldn't keep the smile from her face. "You look the same as always, perfect."

"I hope I'm accepted. I doubt I will be, but there's only one way to find out for certain." He smiled. "Let's go. Shall we walk?"

"I think that's best."

The wind whistled through the branches of the tree-tops as they walked below them. It was a heavenly moment, walking beside Carter. It felt like the breeze was buzzing with thousands of tiny voices telling her she'd made the right choice. She looked up at the gray cloudy sky just as the mid-morning sunlight tried to poke through, making bright outlines on the edges of the clouds.

"It's so beautiful in the orchard. No wonder you love it."

"I do. I don't know how things are going to work

out when I leave the community, but I think things will be okay. No one else can manage the orchard."

"Maybe it'll all work out perfectly. After we marry, we can stay on in the cottage and you can work the orchard. It's not as though you'll have far to travel to work either. It'd be ideal."

"No one else is interested in the orchard, not like I am. My sisters just want to get married, and I'm sure they'll do that and move away. They won't give this place a second thought."

"Right at this moment, your family needs the income from the orchard, right?"

"Yes."

"Well, we certainly don't need the money. You could run the orchard and they could have the proceeds if that's okay with you."

She stared at him. "We have money?"

"I told you I'm comfortable. Now, we're comfortable."

"I don't know what that means." She'd always been the one in charge. She'd made all the financial decisions for the family and when she married Carter, it would be an adjustment.

"We're rich, Florence."

She gulped. "Rich?" She'd never *not* had to worry about every last dollar.

He nodded and then chuckled. "Who knew a childhood hobby would make me millions?"

"Chess?"

"Yes, that's what started it. I got in at the right time too. I've made secure investments and we're set for the rest of our lives."

"God willing," she added.

"Neither of us ever has to work again, but I will because it keeps me occupied, and I know you'll always want to have your trees."

"So, I could work the orchard and the money could go to Wilma and the girls?"

"Yes. Anything you want."

"I like the sound of that and I think they would too. I'd be helping them and doing what I love at the same time. I'm sure Wilma would be fine with that." That solved everything.

"It's nice to see the worry leave your face."

She smiled at him. She was still worried. Worried about their next few days, and weeks, and months.

CHAPTER 2

When she saw the house, she noticed the visiting buggy. "Someone's at the house."

"Is that a bad thing?" he asked.

"It is if we want to talk to Wilma in private, without anybody interfering."

"Who is it?"

She stopped, squinted hard at the distant buggy, and then sighed. "It's Levi Bruner. He's a man who's interested in my mother."

"Shall we leave this for another day, then?"

She looked up into his eyes. "I don't really want to, not when we've come this close."

"Good, that's what I was hoping you'd say because this has been left long enough. We need our relationship out in the open. Who knows, I might get along great with Wilma."

"I hope so. But I feel uncomfortable talking about

this in front of Levi. It really should only be family present when we tell her."

He took both her hands and held them. "What do you suggest?"

"What if I tell her there's someone who wants to speak with her at ten o'clock tomorrow morning? And speak with her with no other visitors around? I'll take her in the buggy and drive her to your place. How does that sound?"

He let go of one of her hands to rub his chin. "I just don't want something to go wrong. What if you disappear and I don't see you for months?"

"I won't do that."

"You've done that to me once before."

"Believe me, I want this as much as you, and I'm ready now. There'll be nothing that'll stand in our way. I'm prepared to leave the community for you, don't forget. Let me say that again, I am leaving the community for you."

"I know, and I appreciate that. And for that reason, we'll do things in your timing."

"Good, and my timing is ten o'clock tomorrow morning. I'll bring her to your place. I won't tell her anything and she won't know where she's going."

He nodded. "Okay."

"I'm sure she thought about you and her sister every day since she found out Iris was pregnant."

"In a positive light I hope, and not in a negative way."

"No, not negative. She misses her sister very much. I can see it when she talks about her."

"Okay, it's a date for ten tomorrow morning. Does that mean I won't see you until then?"

She nodded. "Most likely. I've got so many things to do today."

He pulled her in to himself for a kiss. With his soft lips on hers, she felt giddy. There was a lifetime ahead of her with this man and all of his kisses and affection. She was glad she'd waited, and hadn't gone searching too hard for an Amish husband. God must've had a plan, a plan for her to marry Carter, and that was why she'd been overlooked by the young Amish men in her youth.

Slowly, she stepped back and then pulled her hands away from his. "I'll see you tomorrow."

...

SHE LEFT him and walked to the house, not happy with the fact that Levi Bruner was at the house – again. His visits had grown more frequent. It's not that she didn't like him. He was okay, but she didn't want anybody to replace her father. That was being childish and selfish, but she couldn't help it.

Wilma and her father had been very much in love

and Florence didn't want things to change. If she was marrying Carter, though, maybe Wilma deserved some male companionship too.

Carter and she hadn't had much time to talk about the technicalities of her leaving the community. There were no timelines set and neither was there a wedding date.

One thing she was fairly certain of, as soon as she announced she was leaving, she'd have to find another place to live. Without being baptized, she wouldn't be shunned – officially – from her community, but that didn't mean she wouldn't be unofficially shunned by those people who turned their backs on her.

It was her fondest hope that Wilma would allow her to stay there until she married Carter. On the other hand, the house and the orchard was her father's, so didn't that mean she was entitled to stay? She'd never had that conversation with Wilma because she'd never had the need.

THE CLOSER SHE got to the house, the louder the laughing and the talking from within the house became. The voices belonged to Levi and Wilma.

When Florence walked through the back door of the house, the talking ceased. She opened the door of the kitchen to see Levi and her stepmother at the kitchen table. There was movement as though they'd been sitting close and moved apart when they heard her. Both of them looked uncomfortable.

"Hello, Levi," Florence said, fixing a smile on her face.

He bounded to his feet. "I was just going."

"No need. Do stay and talk to *Mamm*. I've got plenty of things to do in the barn. We are getting a feed delivery tomorrow and I need to rearrange a few things to make room." She looked at her mother. "Can you set aside some time tomorrow morning? There's somewhere I want to take you."

"That's fine."

"We'll leave here about ten in the morning. Will that be all right with you?"

"*Jah*. What is it?"

"I can't tell you."

"It's a surprise?"

Florence opened her mouth wondering what to say. It could certainly be classed as a surprise. "Sort of."

Wilma raised her eyebrows. "I like surprises."

"I hope you'll like this one. It's not exactly a surprise."

Levi sat back down. "I could stay a few more minutes."

"Please do," *Mamm* said. "I'll put the kettle on for a cup of something to warm you."

"*Denke*, Wilma."

When Florence saw them smiling sweetly at one another, and all the love oozing from Levi, she had to leave. She headed out to the barn. She wasn't sure exactly what day the feed was coming, but it had given her a perfect excuse to get out of the house. And she did need to reorganize the barn.

Light flooded the darkness of the barn when she opened the double doors. The clouds of earlier had parted, making way for some late winter sunlight. She got to work and pulled the last few bags of feed to one side so they could be used first. Then she took a broom and swept the floor. It was a chore usually assigned to one or two of the girls, but it didn't hurt to help them out.

When she'd finished, she sat down on a hay bale and thought about what had happened between her and Carter.

She'd made a momentous decision and was on the verge of a new life. A life where she'd never feel alone. Now there was someone special in her life, someone special who loved her.

The only thing was, it was odd to have nothing planned out. Normally, she knew what she'd be doing from day to day and the pattern repeated daily, weekly, every month. The only thing that changed unpredictably was the timing of the seasons.

Now, nothing was planned and she didn't know for certain what tomorrow would bring. Nor did she know what all her tomorrows with Carter would be like. She hoped they'd be filled with love, children, and happiness.

In saying *yes* to Carter she'd taken a risk.

Somehow, though, it didn't seem like she was taking a giant leap of faith, because there was such peace in her heart. The peace of God was reassuring her that He'd still be with her, even though that was against everything she'd been raised to believe.

FLORENCE THOUGHT *Mamm* had forgotten about the upcoming surprise because she'd mentioned nothing throughout dinner. When the younger girls had gone to bed and Florence and Wilma stayed up late sewing, Wilma finally raised the subject. "Can you give me a hint of what the surprise is tomorrow?"

"I can't give you a hint, not without telling you outright. You'll just have to wait and see. It's not an actual thing, like a gift. It's not something you can pick up. Well, I suppose you could but it's not really like that."

"You're being so confusing. Are you sure I'll like it? It's not another dog, is it? Because when Cherish comes back that means we'll already have two dogs in the house now that Isaac gave Joy Goldie. You know I'm not fond of having animals living in the house like those two dogs do." She shook her head.

"*Nee,* it's not a pet. Nothing like a pet."

"Well, we don't need anything else. I don't think I need anything that I can think of. Is it a new dress?"

"*Nee.*" A few minutes later, Florence asked, "Do you want a new dress?"

"Not especially, but I could always do with one. I don't need one, though."

"I'll make you one, then. All you need to do is ask."

"I don't like to ask because you're always so busy doing things for other people."

Florence smiled, glad to have a little recognition for all she did. "I like sewing. I'll make you a dress. How about I take you tomorrow after the surprise, and we can get you some fabric for the dress."

"No need. I've got material here."

She knew *Mamm* was talking about the yards and yards of the same-colored fabric that they often made their everyday dresses out of. All the girls were bored with it, but not *Mamm*. Or at least she'd never said so. "I think we should have something new, don't you?"

"I don't like to spend the money when we've got material here."

"We can afford it."

"Can we?"

"*Jah,* we can."

"I never know. I never know how much money we have because you handle all that kind of thing and before you did it, your *vadder* kept the books."

"We're doing okay. We're more than just surviving. We've had some good years."

"That would've made your *vadder* happy. We had some troubled times during those years back when he had to sell off the piece of the land with our guest *haus* on it. It was convenient for when we had visitors."

Florence nodded, knowing that was the land Carter had bought directly from the people to whom *Dat* had sold it. "I know, I remember that. He was sad about it, but he didn't have much choice."

"That's what he said."

"So, it's settled. We'll shop tomorrow. We won't decide what the color will be or anything. We'll just go there and see what Mrs. Bennett has in her store."

Mamm's face brightened. "I'd like that. *Denke,* Florence. That's something to look forward to. Something else to look forward to apart from the surprise that's not a surprise."

"*Gut*. And I'm not giving out any more hints." Florence giggled.

As Florence sat there sewing in front of the fire, she wondered where Wilma's relationship with Levi was headed. She didn't feel it was right for her to ask.

CHAPTER 3

"Do I need to dress up for the surprise?" *Mamm* asked Florence over breakfast the next morning.

What she meant was, should she wear her Sunday best, which was marginally better than her everyday dresses.

"You'll be fine just how you are. It's not really a surprise," she told Wilma for about the twentieth time.

"Where are you going?" Joy asked as she buttered her toast.

"Florence is taking me somewhere for a surprise."

Florence rolled her eyes. What was the use?

"Where?" the two younger girls chorused. They both giggled and then all eyes were on Florence.

"If I told you, it wouldn't be a surprise." Now she too was starting to call it a surprise, which was bad because Wilma would not only meet her nephew, she'd also find out her sister had died. "*Mamm* will find out first and then she can tell all of you." She looked over at her stepmother. "It's not all super-good. I don't want you to get your hopes up."

"I bet I know what it is," said Favor.

Florence shook her head. "I don't think anyone would possibly know what it is."

"I think I do."

"What is it?" asked Hope.

Favor shook her head. "I'm not going to tattle."

Hope stared at Florence. "Is Cherish coming back?"

"*Jah,* that would be the best surprise of all," Hope added.

"*Nee,* it's not Cherish. She's still with Aunt Dagmar."

"And still being punished, poor thing," Favor said. "It's not fair how you can punish her for so long."

Florence said, "Last time I talked to her, she sounded happy to be staying with Aunt Dagmar, helping her on the farm and all."

"That's not what she said when she was here. She hates it there. It's so isolated and she never gets to talk to anybody except the stupid bird, Timmy."

"I'm sure he's a lovely bird," Florence said.

"She said it's a blue budgerigar and she hates it."

Mamm finally spoke. "And blue budgerigars are delightful, and she has her dog there for company."

"That's right," said Florence. "If we were really punishing her that bad, we wouldn't have allowed her to take Caramel with her."

"That would've been too cruel," Joy said. "I'm glad you let her take Caramel. I would hate to be parted from Goldie."

"That's only because Isaac gave him to you," Favor said before she stuck out her tongue.

"Did you see what she did to me just then, Florence?"

"*Jah*, I did. Can't we just have a nice breakfast where we talk about nice things and behave with patience toward one another?"

They all nodded their heads while Joy sighed. "I suppose the next time Cherish will be back will be for my wedding."

"And when will that be?" Florence wondered if Joy and Isaac had already made a date for the wedding.

"A year or two, I guess."

Florence was pleased to hear that. She looked down at her scrambled egg and buttered toast, and now the thought of eating it made her sick. She was so nervous about how her stepmother would react when she learned Carter was Iris's son. It was one thing to tell her that Carter was her sister's son, but there was so much more she didn't know. Her sister was dead, and that would come as a shock. Also, she'd have to find out sooner or later that Florence was leaving the community to be with Carter.

Somehow, Florence knew it wouldn't all go smoothly. When she felt Wilma looking at her, she quickly piled her fork high with food and popped it into her mouth as though she didn't have a care in the world.

JUST BEFORE TEN O'CLOCK, *Mamm* was at the door and waiting. "I'm ready now Florence."

"*Gut.* I've hitched the buggy and it's waiting." Florence pulled on her black over-bonnet and black cape. Then she held the door open for her stepmother.

As they walked to the buggy, *Mamm* said, "I've been lying awake all night wondering what the surprise could be."

Florence was lost for words. *Mamm* climbed into the buggy and then Florence sat beside her.

"Well, you won't have to wait much longer." Florence picked up the reins and moved her horse onward. "It's not all good, it's mixed with bad. I won't say more than that. Don't get too excited. I think you'll be pleased with part of it, though. Then there's another part that you won't be pleased about."

Mamm frowned. "Are we going far?"

"No. Not far at all." She moved the horse onto the road and then traveled a little distance before she pulled into the very next driveway.

Mamm looked around and then stared at Florence. "Why are we going here? Florence, did we have enough money to buy this place back?"

Her mother looked so excited she hated to disappoint her. "*Nee, Mamm,* I'm sorry. The way the property prices have shot up, we'll never have enough money to buy this place back." When she stopped the buggy, her stepmother was still looking at her with a curious expression on her face. "There is someone in the house for you to meet."

"You want me to meet the neighbor you have a crush on?"

Florence wasn't happy the way Ezekiel had announced to everyone that she was flirting with the neighbor. She didn't speak.

Wilma looked around as she stepped down from the buggy. "This can't be the surprise, meeting the neighbor."

"Just wait and see."

Florence walked up to the door and knocked on it with Wilma just a little way behind her.

"What's his name?" Wilma whispered.

"Carter Braithwaite." She scrutinized her step-mother to see if she'd show any recognition of the name, but she didn't. Carter opened the door and immediately Florence felt more relaxed. He looked even more handsome in a black pullover that showed off his smooth skin. He smiled at Florence and then turned his attention to Wilma.

"You must be Wilma?"

"I am."

"*Mamm*, this is Carter Braithwaite."

"Please come in and sit down." He showed them into his small living room and they sat down in the two-seater couch and he sat opposite them. She could see the anticipation on Carter's face and she knew she had to be the one to speak.

"There's something about Carter that you should know. He moved here because his mother was raised around these parts." She stared at Wilma hoping her mother would figure out who he was.

"That's nice. And where were you living before this, Carter?"

"Here and there." Slowly he rubbed his palms together and then put them down on his lap. "The thing is, it's best that I just tell you straight out." He ran a hand over his cropped hair. "My mother was Iris, your sister."

Wilma bounded to her feet, took a step back and looked at Florence and then stared at Carter. "You're saying that you are Iris's son?"

He stood and then Florence was the only one left seated, so she stood too.

"Yes, she only ever had one child and that was me. When she left your community, she married my father, Gerald Braithwaite."

Wilma muttered under her breath. "I know." She looked at Florence. "The one who wrote that letter. Why would you delve into all that, Florence? This is your doing. Where's Iris? Is she here?" She looked around about her.

He shook his head. "I'm sorry to tell you that my mother died a few years ago."

All color drained from Wilma's face and she sat back down. "She died?"

Florence sat down with her and placed a hand on her stepmother's shoulder.

"Yes, I'm sorry. She did." He sat back down, too.

Mamm covered her mouth and all she could do was stare at Carter. "You look so much like her." She blinked back tears. "Florence, you brought me here and your *surprise* is that my sister is dead?"

"No, *Mamm*. That's not … Carter is your nephew."

She looked at Florence and then at Carter. "I'm sorry I have to go." She hurried out of the house and got into the buggy.

Florence didn't know what to do. She got to the door and turned around. "I'm sorry. It's a lot for her to take in."

"I understand. Go and make sure she's alright. We can talk later."

"I will." She wanted to kiss him goodbye or at least touch him, but he stood there making no move toward her, so she hurried out the door to help Wilma. She knew from Carter's face that he felt rejected.

Florence climbed up to the buggy to see Wilma crying like she had never cried before. "I'm so sorry, Wilma. I never would've—"

"Just take me home," she managed to say.

Florence turned the buggy around and headed back down the driveway. "I feel awful. It was supposed to be a nice surprise for you to meet Iris's son."

"Florence, she's dead. Iris died outside the faith and I'll never see her again. I can never tell her I'm sorry. She died with hardness in her heart toward me, I just know it."

"But … we don't know what was in her heart, though. She could've returned to God."

"But she didn't, Florence. That's just it, she didn't."

"You don't know that for sure, *Mamm*." Florence licked her lips, trying to make a case for Iris following God outside of the community. "How do you know she ever left *Gott?*"

"She would've told me. That's why she kept away from me. Because she knew she wasn't right with *Gott* and she kept away from me."

"I'm sorry, *Mamm,*" she mumbled again. "We were heading to the house to tell you yesterday when we saw Levi was visiting. It wasn't a good time, so Carter and I decided to tell you this morning."

"It's not your fault, Florence. I will visit that young man again soon, in a couple of days. He is my nephew. I should …"

"*Jah,* he's your nephew."

She wiped her eyes. "*Denke,* Florence."

"I'm sorry, I don't know what I was thinking telling you it was a surprise. It was a bad surprise. A terrible one. I'm so stupid sometimes."

Mamm tried to compose herself. "It was my fault. I think I wanted it to be a surprise. With your *vadder* gone, no one ever surprises me anymore. I miss that.

28

Anyway, you were right. It was both good and bad. At least now I know some of what happened to Iris, and after I talk to him again, I'll find out a lot more."

"*Jah,* you will."

"Funny how he came to be our neighbor."

"I'm sure he can tell you about that too."

"Florence, are you telling me everything he told you?"

Florence looked over at her stepmother. "That's all he said. I guess there's more. A lot more he can tell you over time."

"That's not what I meant. Is there something … Never mind."

CHAPTER 4

"CARTER IS the man you have a crush on?"

Florence hadn't intended to talk to Wilma any further about Carter or Iris since she was so upset, but since *Mamm* had asked … "It's a little more than that."

Mamm stared at her. "What do you mean by, 'a little more?'"

"He and I are very close."

"How close?"

Florence felt her heart beating hard. She was concerned it might be too much for Wilma to hear all this news at once. "He's asked me to marry him."

Wilma was silent and her brown eyes opened wide. After a moment, she said, "And you agreed to that?"

"I did. I've never felt like this before."

"Is he speaking to the bishop about joining our community?"

"*Nee*, he's not," she said bluntly. There was no other way to say it.

"But that means you'll have to leave to be with him."

Florence turned the horse into their driveway. "I know that. I haven't made this decision lightly. I've given it a lot of thought."

"I can't believe you'd do that, Florence. You would leave us? No one knows how to run the orchard like you do."

Once they reached the barn, Florence pulled up the horse and held the reins tightly in her hands causing her knuckles to turn white. "We'll work something out." It was her dearest wish that she could stay on and run her apple orchard, but that would be incredibly difficult if her family turned their backs on her.

"I don't know how."

She turned to face Wilma. "You've had a shock about your *schweschder*. Why don't you just let all that sink in before you start thinking about other things?"

"I'd rather know now. What else is there to tell me? You're not pregnant, are you?"

Florence gasped. How could her stepmother think something like that? "*Nee*, of course I'm not."

"Well, that's something at least. I don't know what to think about you anymore, and I'm feeling a headache coming on."

Florence knew their planned trip to town that afternoon to buy fabric might not happen. If she spent more time with Wilma before the girls found out, she'd feel more comfortable. "How about I make you a cup of hot tea and then after we have something to eat, I can take you into town to buy that material?"

"I don't want a new dress," Wilma snapped. "What I want is things to stay how they were. I wish you never met that man from next door."

Florence sat still while Wilma got out of the buggy. *Mamm* was changing her mind fast.

Then with both hands on the buggy door, Wilma glared at her. "How can we know for certain he is who he says he is?"

"He'd have no reason to lie about it. And how would anybody know that you had a *schweschder* called Iris? I didn't even know."

"People can find these things out."

Florence felt her throat constrict and she could barely get words out. "What purpose would it serve?"

"Oh Florence, you have an answer for everything." After she looked at Florence through slitted eyes, she walked to the house. Florence continued to sit there in the buggy staring after her. Now her life was even more awkward and complicated, but it was going to be worth it when she was with Carter.

She unhitched the buggy and turned the horse out into the paddock, then walked inside and headed to the kitchen.

Wilma walked straight past her. "I'm heading to bed, I have a nasty headache coming along."

"I'm sorry, *Mamm.* No one meant to give you a headache."

"I'll be alright. I will. It brought back a lot of bad memories and I thought I'd never have to face some things again. Thanks to you, I do."

Florence wasn't sure she understood. "Let me know if you need anything."

As Wilma walked up the stairs she looked down at Florence. "Just look after the girls, will you? And don't tell them what you told me. I don't want them to know about Carter. Not just yet. It'll crush them."

Florence couldn't agree to that. "I've left things too long already. They'll need to know and I'm telling them today."

Wilma made no comment and walked up the stairs.

Florence walked into the kitchen, boiled the teakettle again, and made herself a cup of strong coffee. She sat down alone at the kitchen table and wished *Mamm* had been more accepting of Carter.

WHEN THE GIRLS came home two hours later, there had been no sight of Wilma. Florence took it upon herself to sit her stepsisters down and she told them she would soon be leaving the community. When they asked her one hundred and one questions, she realized how silly the whole thing must've sounded to them. She and Carter didn't even have a plan. For the first time in her life, things weren't organized and mapped out. *The details can look after themselves.* She trusted *Gott* that this was what she was meant to do.

"Are you sure this is what you want?" asked Favor, the second youngest.

"I wouldn't leave the community just because I felt like it. This is true love."

"How can it be true love though?" Joy asked. "He's not one of us, and how can you be in love with him when he doesn't really know who you are? He can't know who you are because he doesn't understand us, our ways, or who we are."

"I think Florence knows what she's doing. She's never liked anybody before."

Florence was surprised by Hope's comments. *"Denke,* Hope."

"When did you know things weren't going to work out with Ezekiel?" asked Joy.

"He was nice and everything, but he just didn't seem a good fit."

"And what would you know?" Favor said, nudging her sister's shoulder.

"I'd know a lot more than you."

"Keep the noise down, I told you *Mamm* has a headache." As soon as she mentioned her stepmother, she knew she had to tell the girls of Carter's identity, that he was really their cousin. "There's another thing you should know," Florence said.

"What about?" Joy asked.

"It's about Carter."

From the bottom of the stairs *Mamm's* voice interrupted, "That's quite enough, Florence."

She turned around to see her stepmother holding a washcloth over her forehead. "*Mamm*, are you feeling any better?"

"*Nee*. And all I could hear from my bed is raised voices. Would you keep the noise level down?"

"It was Hope," Favor said.

"*Nee*, it wasn't. It was all of you. I could hear every last one of you."

"I was just telling them that I'll be leaving. Sorry if we were too loud," Florence said.

"Your mind's made up?"

"*Jah*, it is. And I was just about to tell them the other news about Carter."

"Florence Baker, I think you've told them quite enough upsetting news for one day. I don't think you should be filling their heads with nonsense."

"I wasn't, I was just about to tell them what *you* should tell them."

"Stop it, Florence. What are you trying to do to me?"

Florence saw that her half-sisters were just as shocked at *Mamm's* reaction as she was.

Mamm spoke again, a little more calmly, "I'll have news of my own to tell everybody tomorrow. Until then, nobody will be telling any more stories. Now I'm going back to bed and everybody please whisper."

"Can I bring you anything, *Mamm*?" Joy asked.

"Nee!" *Mamm* marched back up the stairs.

Favor leaned in to Florence and whispered, "What was it you were about to tell us?"

"I can't tell you now. It sounds like *Mamm* wants to tell you tomorrow."

"It must be pretty important," Joy said.

"It's very interesting. But I can't give you any hints or tell you what it is, so please don't ask me. That horse feed delivery hasn't come yet. Wasn't it supposed to be here by now?"

"Larry's running a day behind. We passed him in town."

"Oh, good to know. Then he'll be here tomorrow?"

"Yes, he should be."

CHAPTER 5

FLORENCE DIDN'T SEE her stepmother until the next morning when she was cooking eggs and bacon for the girls. Everyone turned around and looked at *Mamm* when she walked into the room.

"Are you feeling better today, *Mamm?*"

"I am." She sat down with the girls. "Florence, I need to tell you that I've been giving it a lot of thought and I don't want to ever see that man from next door again."

Florence stared at *Mamm,* devastated, while the bacon sizzled in the pan.

"Don't burn it, Florence. I don't like my bacon black," Hope said.

Florence flipped the bacon over and noticed one side was already quite brown. "You'll have it how it comes."

"*Nee.* I don't like it unless it's well done and crispy,"

Favor complained.

"I'm not going to cook the bacon five different ways for five different people." Florence took the pan off the stove and switched off the gas.

"Sorry," Hope called out loudly.

Joy jumped up to help carry the five plates to the breakfast table.

"I need another cup of *kaffe*, Florence," Favor announced just as Florence had sat down.

"Then, I suggest you get it for yourself."

Favor's mouth dropped open. "Rude."

"She's not being rude," Joy said. "She's just made you breakfast, so the least you can do is get your own second cup of *kaffe*."

Favor got up to get it herself. "Does anyone else want one?"

"I'll have one." *Mamm* held up an empty mug. "Florence didn't even get me my first one this morning."

Florence ignored that remark. Why would she get *Mamm* her coffee when she was still in bed? That was when the girls got their first ones – before her stepmother had come downstairs. The important issue was that the girls still didn't know that Carter was their cousin. She'd talk to *Mamm* about that later. Surely, she'd see sense and realize that the girls had a right to know their cousin was living next door to them?

"What did the man next-door do apart from being in love with Florence?" Joy asked looking between *Mamm* and Florence.

Florence shrugged. "He did nothing wrong at all. You'll have to ask *Mamm* if you want to know anything else."

"Well, *Mamm*? Florence said she's leaving for him."

"Just be quiet and eat your breakfast and no talking about Florence and that man to anybody."

Favor sighed as she handed *Mamm* her coffee. "I hate secrets."

"That's because you like to flap your gums," Hope said with a giggle.

"I still have a headache and I don't want to talk about the man next door ever again."

Favor sat down with her second cup. "Well, what's happening today?"

"We've got the feed delivery coming and then after you do your chores, you can have a free afternoon." Florence finally took her first mouthful of breakfast. Even though she wasn't hungry with all the conflict going on around her, she knew she had to keep up her strength.

"Finally!" Hope said.

Mamm stared at Hope. "You've been having lots of free time lately."

"*Jah*, but we've been so busy with having so much to do."

Mamm took a sip of coffee and then set the mug down. "I've been thinking that it's time that we get Cherish back home. We've all missed her so much."

The girls all agreed with enthusiasm, while Florence

sat struggling through her meal in silence. The only reason *Mamm* wanted Cherish back was because *Mamm* was angry with Florence. That was one thing Florence knew for certain.

"When is she coming back?" Favor asked. "I'll have to get my things out of her room."

"I'll have Florence make the arrangements." She looked over at Florence and for the first time that morning, made eye-contact. "Can you do that after breakfast, Florence?"

"If that's what you want, *Mamm*. I will arrange for a driver to bring her home."

"I can't wait," Joy said. "I hope Caramel gets along with Goldie."

Florence knew there was no point protesting about Cherish coming home. She smiled at Joy. "I'm sure he will. The two of them can play together."

"Not in the *haus*," *Mamm* said. "I don't want dogs running through the place. If it's too much ruckus, we might have to give one of the dogs away."

"*Nee*," said Joy. "If Goldie goes, I go."

"It's just a dog," *Mamm* said.

"He's not just a dog, he's my dog. What's more, Isaac gave him to me. He's like my *boppli*."

Mamm rolled her eyes and shook her head. "There's no need to be so dramatic. You're sounding like Cherish."

"Yeah, well just don't send me away."

"I won't have to if you behave yourself."

The place should've been peaceful, but it never was. Florence longed for the day she'd be married to Carter. She could have a peaceful happy home and she'd raise her children in a way that they wouldn't misbehave – ever.

AFTER FLORENCE HAD DONE her chores, and made the arrangements for Cherish to come home, she couldn't wait to see Carter. She raced through the orchard and when his house came into view, she saw him sitting on the porch. He must've noticed her because he stood up and started walking toward her. They met at the fence line. After he helped her through the fence, they embraced with a warm hug. It always felt good to be in his arms where she was warm, safe, and loved.

"How's Wilma?"

"Not too good. The news about her sister gave her a headache. She'll be better soon."

"That's too bad. Are we ready to tell your step-mother about us getting married?"

"I kind of did."

"Did you?"

She nodded. "I did, because she asked, but then she didn't want to talk about it. I mentioned it to the girls too. That's when *Mamm* told them not to mention it to anyone. She also hasn't told them about you being their cousin."

He sighed. "We're getting closer, if you've told them."

"I don't know. It feels like she's ignoring everything."

"That's not good."

"I think we'll have to wait a bit longer."

"No. I'm through with waiting, Florence. Let's just get married."

"I want to do everything peacefully and harmoniously. We will get there, we will be married, but I don't want to do it at the expense of anyone else's happiness."

He nodded. "I understand, it's because of your upbringing. I've done a little reading about the Amish since I found out that's where my mother came from. You're peace-loving people; turn the other cheek and all that. I don't agree, or believe in that kind of thing. I think you see what you want and then you go after it no matter who you have to trample over to get to it."

She giggled. "I don't see you as that kind of a person at all."

"Maybe not. But that's what I strive for." He grinned at her.

"I'll never believe that."

"I hope Wilma gets used to the news." He put his arm around her. "Let's go to the house." He was just the perfect height to rest his arm around her shoulders comfortably.

Once they were inside, he stood still and warmed

himself in front of the roaring fire. She took off her shawl and placed it on the couch on the other side of her.

"Tell me what Wilma said when she left here."

"She was okay at first, and mentioned talking to you more and then something in her mind seemed to snap. Suddenly, she changed her mind. Of course, she was upset that Iris died. She'll never get to apologize or say what she wanted to say. Maybe she thought about that more."

"Is there anything else? I'm sensing you're holding back." He sat down beside her and rubbed her arm.

She blew out a deep breath. "She said she never wants to see you again."

He raised his eyebrows. "That was a reaction I didn't expect. She's my aunt. And she said that after you told her we're getting married?"

"That's right, so after we marry, she might not want to see me either."

"I'm sorry, Florence."

She nodded. "I'm prepared for it. I know some will turn their backs on me."

He rubbed his chin and then looked into the crackling fire. "I have no relatives on my father's side and I only have my mother's side." He looked back at her. "I told you I didn't have anyone and that was a self-fulfilling prophecy."

"That's where you're wrong. You have me now."

"That's right, I do." He took hold of her hand and

interlaced his fingers with hers. "And I don't want to lose you, and that's why I want us to get married as soon as possible. Before you change your mind."

She giggled. "I won't change my mind. I've given you my word."

"I know, but anything can happen and it doesn't stop a man from worrying. I feel you're always out of reach, like we're never quite there. I can't lose you, Florence."

"You won't." She licked her lips. "When do you want to get married?"

"Next week."

She giggled. "We still haven't worked out anything with Wilma about the orchard. I have to have a serious conversation with her about all of that. I think she's blocked out what I've told her about you and me."

"And by the sounds of her at the moment, it doesn't seem like you'll be able to tell her anything else about us."

"It's just an adjustment. It'll only be a few days. I'm sure of it. Soon, she'll want to ask you about her sister. I'm sure of it." She smiled at him.

He shook his head. "I'll wait a few days if you think that's all it'll take. Any longer than that and I'll come to your house, throw you over my shoulder and take you away with me."

She put a hand over her mouth and giggled. "You would, wouldn't you?"

"I would, and I will."

"It'll only take a few days. Cherish is coming back tomorrow. I've arranged for a driver to pick her up early in the morning so she should be home by afternoon."

"Why's she coming back?"

"I'm not sure. *Mamm* just announced this morning that she wanted her to come home. I think it'll be a good distraction for *Mamm*. And then she might feel more relaxed about accepting you. Then we can talk about our marriage and sort out something about the orchard."

"I understand you want to keep your orchard, but I can buy us another orchard. Just remember that, if things don't go your way – which I'm inclined to think they won't."

"Thank you, that's a very generous offer."

"I'm being practical. I know you want your orchard because of the sentimental value attached to it, but if it doesn't work out we'll just steal a couple of trees and take them with us."

She giggled. "That's funny."

He laughed. "It might be, but I wasn't joking. You deserve to take a few trees if it comes to that."

"Oh, don't worry, I'll be taking my father's special trees – the rare ones. No one else will want them and they're not that large." She shook her head. "I'm sure they'll be happy with me allowing them to live in the house and have the income from the orchard, and they'll let me run the place."

"I'll have to take your word for that. If it was in the

real-world, people would be fighting you tooth-and-nail to keep the house, the orchard and all the money."

"'Real world?' Am I living in a fake world?"

"I'm sorry, I shouldn't have said that – not that way. I meant in the non-Amish world."

Florence didn't say anything, but the way he thought of his world being so different from hers highlighted the differences between them. As much as she loved him and didn't want to be without him, she hoped she wasn't about to make a big mistake.

"You're prepared to leave your community, as you said?"

"I am and I will. I've told my family how I feel about you. That's huge for me."

"Why don't we make one small step?"

"What did you have in mind?"

"Come shopping with me tomorrow and we'll buy you some clothes. Some non-Amish ones."

She thought about that for a moment. "I couldn't wear jeans or men's clothes."

"Well, they aren't men's clothes when they're made for women to wear them, are they?"

Florence winced. It would take her a while to get some things out of her head.

"You don't have to wear anything you're not comfortable with."

She nodded. "I can do that."

"Good. That shows me we're getting closer to our goal."

"Only thing is, so much is happening tomorrow with my sister coming home. Can we do it the day after?"

"Sure. Come over early and we'll make a day of it. I'll take you to lunch somewhere nice."

"Okay. I'll look forward to it."

"Not as much as I will."

She smiled at him. "I should go. I don't want *Mamm* to start worrying about me."

He bounded to his feet, held his hands out and pulled her up.

They walked out of the house and when they got to the fence, he held the wires apart for her to slip through. They shared a kiss over the fence.

"I'll see you tomorrow?" he asked.

"I think so, just briefly though, with Cherish coming home, but I'll definitely look forward to our day together."

"Me too. Bye, Florence."

"Bye."

She made her way back through the orchard feeling better about things. He always gave her hope. It was good to be wanted and to have those same feelings in return. She'd never felt anything for Ezekiel except thinking that he was a nice person. If she'd married Ezekiel, she would've made the best of it. Now that she knew what true love was, she could never settle for less and was pleased she'd never have to.

CHAPTER 6

IT WAS JUST after two o'clock the next day when Cherish arrived.

Florence saw the car coming while she was cleaning one of the upstairs bedroom windows. "She's here," she called out.

Favor started shrieking, and Florence hurried downstairs. Joy had her dog, Goldie, in her arms ready to meet Caramel.

Mamm started crying before the car even got to the house. "What's wrong, *Mamm?*" Joy asked.

"I'm just pleased to have her back."

"I'm sure she's pleased to be back, too," Hope said, and then she pulled on *Mamm's* sleeve. "I've been meaning to ask about my pen pal coming to stay. She's a nice girl living in Texas."

"I can't think about that now, Hope." *Mamm* shook her head.

"She can't have a pen pal come to stay. I've had pen pals a lot longer than she has, and mine have never been allowed to stay."

"So what?"

"It's only right mine should come to stay first."

"Shush all of you, or *Mamm* will send you both to Aunt Dagmar's, isn't that right, *Mamm?*" Joy said.

"It is tempting sometimes."

Florence giggled to herself just as the car pulled up outside the house. The back door of the car opened and Caramel jumped out and ran toward the house just as Joy put her dog down. The two of them stared at each other, and then circled each other, sniffing as they went. Then they started jumping at each other, and then they ran off together. Cherish stood beside the car staring at the dogs.

"Whose dog's that?"

"It's my dog," Joy said. "I wrote to you about him."

"I don't remember getting a letter about a dog."

"Isaac gave him to me. I wrote about it in the same letter that I told you that Isaac and I were getting married."

"I remember reading that part, but I don't remember reading the part about the dog. I was probably just so pleased for you about getting married because no one ever thought you would."

Joy put her hands on her hips. "And why's that?"

"Forget it. Where have the dogs gone?"

"I hope they don't run about all crazy inside the *haus*," *Mamm* said.

Cherish then ran to her mother and hugged her. "*Denke* for letting me come back. I was fine there, though. I'm getting quite used to it. Can I go back soon?"

"You want to go back there?" *Mamm* looked over at Florence, horrified at what Cherish had said.

Florence said nothing and hurried over to pay the driver. It was the same driver they'd used a few times before. She listened to the conversation between *Mamm* and Cherish as she handed over the money.

"I do want to go back," Cherish said, "And she needs me there. She'll miss me."

Joy said, "You can't be serious, Cherish. You're always complaining about it and how much you hate it."

"I didn't really mean it." Cherish laughed. "You'll believe anything. I like it there. Maybe I'll stay here, I don't know. I'll see if you're all nice to me."

She hugged her sisters and then stepped forward and said to Florence, "Aren't you going to hug your youngest *schweschder?*"

Florence was pleased that she didn't say half-*schweschder*. "Of course. Welcome home." Florence leaned down and embraced her. *Mamm* and all the girls were considerably shorter than she, which also helped make her feel the odd one out. Their eyes were either

53

brown or hazel, and hers were bright blue just like her father's.

"How's Timmy, the annoying bird?" Favor asked her.

"He's okay. I'm trying to help teach him to talk."

"Let's have something to eat," Florence interrupted before the girls started squabbling. "Favor's made chocolate cake."

"Did you, Favor?"

Favor nodded.

"That's my favorite, *denke.*"

"Mine too," said Hope.

The girls all made their way into the kitchen while they left the dogs to dart about outside. *Mamm* was quick to close the door on the dogs once all the girls were inside. When they were halfway through the chocolate cake, they heard the grinding wheels of a wagon and the clip-clop of hooves.

"That'll finally be Larry with the feed delivery. Only a day later than he said." Florence walked outside and yelled over her shoulder, "I need some help."

To her surprise, her four sisters left what they were doing and came outside to help her. Larry was there with his young employee, Tom. Florence opened the barn doors and told the girls where to instruct Larry and his worker to put things. She had intended to go back inside and talk with *Mamm* about Carter, but stopped when she saw Tom and Cherish talking. She knew from the way Cherish was acting, all coy and twirling her *kapp* strings around her fingers, that she liked Tom. Only problem was, Tom was soon to marry Isabel. Not only that, Tom seemed just as pleased to be talking with Cherish.

Florence decided not to say anything for now, but it was in the back of her mind that Cherish was better off at Aunt Dagmar's. Cherish was too much for her to handle and she was definitely too much for *Mamm*.

Florence didn't go inside as planned, but stayed close to Cherish the whole time. When the delivery had been completed, Larry's wagon rattled back down the driveway. Florence shut the barn doors, and then called Cherish over while the other girls walked to the house. As much as Florence thought she should keep quiet about what she'd just seen, she couldn't.

"What is it, Florence?" Cherish asked.

"What did you say to Tom just now?"

"Nothing much." Cherish looked at her, blinking her wide innocent eyes.

"He's quite a bit older than you and I'm just wondering what you had to talk about."

She shrugged her shoulders. "I don't remember. I was just being polite. It was nothing."

Florence tapped her chin. "It seems you were polite to Tom, but you weren't the same with Larry."

"Larry's old and ugly," Cherish blurted out.

"Ah, I see. So, you're only polite to young handsome men whether they're engaged or not?"

Cherish gasped. "He's engaged?"

"You know very well he is. It was announced just before you left around the time of Honor's wedding."

"If I knew, I must've forgotten. Anyway, I'm not interested in him, so don't worry. As you said, he's far too old for me. Not as old as Larry, but still old. Is there any harm in just talking?"

Florence shook her head. "Let's just forget we had this conversation."

"That suits me just fine and I'll forget about you wanting to marry the *Englisher* next door."

Florence's mouth fell open in shock

"Did you think the girls wouldn't tell me?" Cherish asked.

"It's not a secret. *Mamm* just didn't want people in the community knowing, not just yet."

She leaned in and said to Florence, "It's good to be back."

"It's nice to have you back," Florence replied, through gritted teeth.

Cherish skipped back to the house ahead of Florence. Part of Florence wanted to be young and care-free like Cherish. If only she could turn back the clock. Even if she could go back, she wasn't sure she had the kind of personality to be carefree; not when she had a compulsion for planning every part of her life. Organized people were never carefree. Maybe she could try being without a care for one day, to start with. *Oh, to be tossed about in the wind like a golden autumn leaf, not knowing or caring where the swift breeze would take me ...*

THAT NIGHT they had a surprisingly nice dinner, Isaac was invited, and of course, *Mamm* had invited Ada and Samuel for Cherish's first dinner back home.

Mamm hadn't mentioned anything about Carter at all. Florence went to bed so looking forward to the next day that she was going to spend with Carter. Perhaps, for tomorrow only, she could forget about the girls and the orchard, and be like one of those leaves.

CHAPTER 7

THE NEXT MORNING, when breakfast was over and Florence had washed up, Cherish whined about wanting to be taken into town. Florence wondered if she whined like this at Aunt Dagmar's. Something told Florence she'd saved it all up for when she got home.

"What do you say, Florence?" Cherish stared at her with pleading eyes.

"You'll have to get Joy to take you into town. I'm doing something else today."

Her attention switched to Joy. "Would you take me, Joy?"

"Okay. Where do you want to go?"

"I said I'd meet a couple of my friends at the markets. And I don't want you to come with me to meet them. I want to see them by myself."

Joy just raised her eyebrows.

"I'll go with you, Joy, and keep you company."

"*Denke*, Favor."

"Where are you going Florence?" *Mamm* asked.

"I'm going somewhere with the man next-door."

Everyone stared at Florence as she took off her work apron and folded it.

"I have news of my own to share soon," *Mamm* said, causing everyone to focus their attention on *Mamm*.

"What is it, *Mamm?*" Joy asked.

"Florence thinks she has news about the man next-door, but I have news of my own that I'll tell you girls soon. Maybe even tonight."

"Will you tell me too?" asked Florence before she realized she had to be finally telling them about Carter being Iris's son, and therefore their cousin.

"*Jah*, I'll tell you all."

Florence was relieved. It would be nice for Carter to have family at last. Although, they could never really be close to him. He might come for the occasional meal; they couldn't deny he was a close relative.

"I'll be looking forward to it." With her apron tucked under her arm, Florence spread the damp dish-cloth over the tap to dry.

"What is it with you and the man next-door?" Hope asked.

Cherish tilted her head back. "I was just about to ask the very same thing."

She looked over at *Mamm*. "I told you already and I know you told Cherish. I don't need to repeat it. He's taking me somewhere today."

"You can't be friends with an outsider," Joy said. "Wanting to marry one is even worse."

Florence shot a quick look at *Mamm* to see if she'd say anything. Her stepmother didn't even make eye-contact with her. "He's not exactly an outsider, in a way. He's not a total stranger."

"Is he going to join us?" asked Joy.

"I hope so, but I don't know that for sure. Maybe one day."

Joy shook her head, clearly unhappy. "You know what the scripture says about us being too close to people on the outside."

"*Jah*, I know it just as well as you, and you don't need to worry about that."

"Florence knows what she's doing. She's the most cleverest person I know," Favor said.

Hope rolled her eyes at Favor. "If you weren't asleep in *schul* all the time, you'd know you don't say *most cleverest*."

"What does it matter? You knew exactly what I meant, and I only fell asleep once."

Joy said, "It was three times that I remember. Honor had to keep poking you."

Favor huffed. "I only remember the one time."

"*Jah*, because you slept through the other times."

"I'll get changed into going out clothes, and then I'll see you all sometime tonight." Florence walked away from their back-and-forth chatter, pleased to be getting away from them for the day.

. . .

FLORENCE CHANGED into her best dress, pulled on her black stockings, redid her hair and fixed it into place with pins. She had no idea what kind of clothes Carter would think she ought to wear. As daunting as it was, having new clothes was a small step toward showing Carter that what she'd promised was really going to happen. He deserved that much and a whole lot more.

When she tiptoed downstairs, she could still hear everyone in the kitchen arguing about something. She quietly closed the front door and tried to close all her concerns behind her. The further away she got from the house, the calmer she felt.

As she moved along the dew-dampened orchard floor, she realized she was probably far earlier than Carter might've expected her. He'd said early, but maybe she was too early. She slowed her pace and said a prayer asking God that, if He willed it, she'd be able to keep running her beloved orchard. She stared up at the dull morning sky as gray and white clouds blew gently across it. One thing she couldn't help wondering about was, would God still hear her prayers now that she intended leaving the community? And what about after?

CARTER OPENED his door with a coffee mug in his

hand. "I was just looking out to see if you were coming and here you are."

"I know I'm probably early, but I had to get away. Is that okay?"

"Sure. I'm pleased." He hugged her and then with his free hand, led her through the doorway. Then he closed the door behind him with the back of his foot. "Would you like a cup of coffee?"

"Yes please. I'd love one."

He walked with her to the kitchen. As he fixed the coffee, she sat down on a stool at the island countertop. "What's going on with those bonnet... I mean those sisters of yours?"

"It's impossible sometimes. They're always bickering between themselves about the smallest of things. Often, it's about things that happened years ago. I don't know how they keep track. Maybe, they make it all up. Yes, that's what they must do."

"I suppose that happens in a household full of children. I grew up with a lot of quiet. I would've given anything to have someone to argue with."

"I guess it wouldn't have been so good being an only child. I've always had my older brothers and my younger sisters."

He placed the coffee mug in front of her and then moved around to the other side of the island and sat down next to her. "Sorry I don't have any milk."

"That's okay I just take it black anyway, and no sugar."

"Good, because I don't think I've got any sugar in the house either. Probably because I don't cook, or have visitors who might need sugar in their coffee." He took a sip. "I could get interested in cooking when I have you to cook for."

"No need for that. Unless … you want to learn? I'm happy to do all the cooking."

"Really?"

She nodded. "I love to cook."

"I don't know if I do or not, but I think I'd like cooking together with you. I haven't given much thought to the day-to-day arrangements."

"Me either."

"We both should start thinking about those things. And, speaking of that, is Wilma breaking down her barriers against me?"

She would've liked to give him a better answer. He'd asked casually, but she knew he wanted some kind of acceptance from his aunt. "I'm not sure what's going on in her head. She did say she had something to tell the girls, so I'd reckon she's going to tell them today. They're all going out, so she'll be home by herself now and that'll give her time to think."

"How can you be sure she's going to tell them?"

"She said there was something she wanted to talk with us all about tonight. Hopefully, she'll talk to Ada and she'll make Wilma see sense – Ada's Wilma's best friend." She bit the inside of her mouth. Adding that bit about Ada revealed that Wilma was reluctant in accepting him.

He scratched his head. "I was hoping for her to be more genuine."

"In what way?"

"I'd hoped … I'd hoped she'd welcome me with open arms. I knew, deep down, that she wouldn't. That's why I never made contact."

Florence didn't say anything, but she could feel his pain. She'd lost both of her parents as well and knew how lonely that would've felt without having an extended family around. "She'll tell the girls tonight I'm sure of it. I can't think of anything else she could have to tell them."

He glanced over at her. "That remains to be seen. I'm not holding out any hope." He gave a low chuckle at the situation.

Florence knew it was his way of covering secret pain. He wasn't so different from her.

"Let's not talk about anything that'll make us sad today. Today's about you and me spending our first day together."

She smiled. "That's right. It is."

"How's your coffee?"

"Really good."

CHAPTER 8

ON THE WAY INTO TOWN, he clutched the steering wheel and chuckled. "I never thought this day would come."

"You didn't?"

He shook his head, not taking his eyes off the road.

"I hoped it would."

He glanced over at her and grinned. "Did you now?"

"I felt the connection when we met, but it was something I didn't want to think about because ..."

"Go on, say it."

"Because you're an outsider. Not Amish."

He shrugged. "People are just people. I don't see that religion should separate everyone. There's not enough tolerance."

"But it does separate, and it has to. You want to be with – marry someone who has the same ideas as you, and then you know that your foundation will be strong."

"Just because I'm, 'not Amish,' that doesn't mean I'm a bad person. I still have morals and standards I live by."

There it was again. He openly admitted he didn't believe in God. She didn't know how someone could *not* believe in God. How did they think the world had come into being with its intricate designs in nature, and who orchestrated the seasons and put everything into place?

"I don't blame you for believing in God because you've been raised to believe that way, and you know nothing else. You haven't had the benefit of a college education. That would've helped."

"Carter, that's a dreadful thing to say. I think for myself and I don't need further education to open my eyes to the truth."

"I hope I haven't offended you."

She hoped this wasn't going to be an ongoing problem with them. If only he'd see everything that she saw. "You have. I think for myself."

"I didn't mean it to come across harshly. I just meant that if you've been brought up thinking a certain way and everyone you know thinks and lives that way, you're not going to think any different. You only have one reference point."

She had to be patient with him. Their differences

were bound to surface. She had to trust in God about that. She was certain of her faith. Maybe Carter would see God through her eyes, in time. "There is a God and He's a scientific God – a wonderful master planner. How else could all this have come about? The whole world isn't an accident or an evolution. Even if some of it has evolved, someone had to start it. It had to have a beginning."

He backed his car into a parking space. She knew that if anything could come between them it would be their differing beliefs; she'd already given her word to Carter that she'd marry him and leave the community. But leaving God wasn't part of that. God would work on his heart, isn't that why they'd met?

When he turned off the car's engine, he looked over at her. "I can see why you think that way and I've considered all that. And you could be right, but it is a decision I'm going to have to come to by myself."

She nodded. "Everyone has to come to that decision themselves. No one can be forced. I hope you don't think I was trying to do that. That's just the way I … I just know in my heart and my soul and in my mind that it's true. And I want you to know what I know because it's very important to me."

"Believe me, if you're right and there *is* a God, I want to know Him." He wagged a finger at her. "That doesn't mean I'd turn Amish and live a backward life. I'm sorry, but I could never do that."

"Would you do it for me?"

He lifted up his hands and looked upward. "Here I am, God, if you want me to know you, I'm willing." He promptly dropped his arms, looked over at her and smiled.

She nodded in appreciation of his acknowledgement, but wasn't sure if he was playing along with her or mocking her. Either way, she knew God had heard his words, and He always answered.

"Come on let's go. There's a frock shop not too far up the road."

She giggled. "'Frock shop?'"

"That's what my mother used to call them."

"Good, I can't wait." She got out of the car and together they walked up the street.

She was relieved he didn't try to hold her hand or put his arm around her, because somebody might've taken particular notice of them if he had. She felt conspicuous enough just walking beside him. It would definitely attract too much attention, an Amish woman and an *Englisher* holding hands.

"This is it." He pushed open the glass door and she walked through to be faced with racks upon racks of ready-to-wear clothing.

She froze, wide-eyed, not knowing where to start.

The shop assistant, a woman in her mid-twenties, walked over. "Can I help you with anything?"

"Yes, I'm looking for some clothes. Just some plain clothes."

She looked her up and down. "What style were you thinking of?"

Florence held out her arms. "Nothing like what I'm wearing now. More like something you're wearing."

"Come this way."

She followed the shop assistant while Carter was looking at some things at the front of the store.

The woman pulled some dresses off one of the racks. "How about this one?"

She looked at the blue dress. "I think so." It was plain and simple, although much shorter than she'd been used to wearing. Also, her legs were always covered in black stockings. It would be a change for them to be uncovered, or covered in the nylon hose that *Englischer* women wore with dresses. And then what about shoes? Her Amish boots weren't going to work very well with these clothes!

The saleslady broke into her thoughts. "Would you like to try these on?"

"Yes, I would."

"While you're doing that, I'll find more for you to try."

"Thank you."

Carter suddenly appeared. "Try them on, and then come out and show me."

She giggled. "Okay."

The assistant hung the clothing in the changing room and Florence walked in and closed the door behind her. When she turned around and saw herself in the mirror, she was surprised at how old and plain she looked. She moved closer to the mirror and stared at her pale skin. It was flat and sallow.

What did Carter see in her?

Surely he could have any woman he wanted. It was a mystery. One of the first things she wanted to do when she left the community was wear a little make up. Not too much, just enough to even out her skin tone and give her a little color.

After she'd changed into the first dress, she walked out to show Carter. He was sitting in a chair looking down at his phone. He looked up and placed his phone in his lap.

"I love it. You look great, like I knew you would. What a figure you've got."

She felt the heat rise in her cheeks and she was glad that the shop assistant wasn't anywhere about.

"Take your bonnet off, so I can get the full effect."

She grabbed onto the strings. "I can't do that."

He frowned. "You're not going to keep wearing it when you leave, are you?"

"I won't, but I haven't left yet."

He nodded. "Okay, I can see your point."

The assistant came up with an armful of clothes. "That looks lovely."

She probably says that to everyone. "Do you think so?" Florence asked.

"Yes. And that's a good color for you, too. It makes your eyes light up. I've got more here that I think will suit. If you tell me what you like or dislike, I can choose others more easily."

"Okay thanks. I'll try them on." She looked back at Carter to see that he was still staring at her. "Do we have time?"

"All the time in the world."

Over the next half hour, each time she put something on, she looked in the mirror first and decided if she liked the fit and the color. The saleswoman had given her a clue by mentioning her blue eyes. A few outfits were discarded, but most of them looked pretty good to her. Each time she changed into one she liked, she went out and asked Carter's opinion. He loved everything she showed him.

By the time the shop assistant came back to see if she needed any help, she'd found around six different outfits she and Carter agreed on – three dresses, and several skirt-and-blouse combinations.

"How are you doing? Can I get you any different sizes?"

"I think we're about done for today. We'll take all of them," he said.

"Carter, we only came to get one."

"You'll use them all in time. You can't just have one thing to wear." He looked at the sales assistant. "We'll take a couple of sweaters, too, and a couple of scarves as well. And she'll need some nice everyday shoes that work with these outfits."

"Okay, I'll show them to you."

He looked over at Florence and smiled. "You get changed, first – before we look at shoes – and I'll select a few other things for you."

"Okay." Florence was overwhelmed. She desperately hoped she had enough money to pay. She couldn't let him pay for so much; it wasn't as though they were married yet.

She got changed and carried out her armful of chosen clothes and placed them on the counter. There was more clothing there that the assistant was folding up, sweaters and scarves and nylon stockings, while Carter patiently looked on.

"Is this all mine?"

"Yes, it is. And now we need to have you try on some shoes."

The saleswoman led them to the shoe department, and she tried on a bunch of different styles until she'd found two pair that were the right combination of comfort and style to go with her new wardrobe. As she tried to decide between them, Carter told the assistant to add both boxes to the stack of clothes.

The total came to just over six hundred dollars, and she only had one hundred and fifty with her.

She clutched her purse, embarrassed. "Do you have layaway?"

"Florence, I'm paying for it." He reached into his pocket.

"I can't let you pay for all that. It's too much."

He shook his head at her and pulled out a wad of notes and handed over seven hundred in one hundred dollar notes.

Florence had never seen someone carry that much money. She'd only seen money like that at harvest time. "Are you sure?"

"Of course I'm sure. I'm sure about everything I do."

Florence noticed that the assistant had a wry smile on her lips. And then she looked up at Florence. "Don't complain. I hope he has a brother!"

Florence smiled back at her, and Carter barked a quick laugh.

HE CLOSED ALL the bags into the trunk of the car. "I'm hungry. How about you?"

"I am. It must be lunchtime."

"How do you feel about Italian?" He joined her on the sidewalk.

"Okay. I love Italian food."

"You've had it before?"

"Of course I have."

"I didn't know." He chuckled. "The Italian restaurant is this way. It's nothing flashy, but the food's excellent." As they walked, he added, "I thought you might have only had Amish food. Like whoopee pies and apple pies and apple cider."

She shook her head. "I live in the same world as you. I'll be cooking for you soon enough, and then you'll know about traditional Amish food."

"I can't wait. It'll give my microwave a rest."

She laughed.

CHAPTER 9

THEY SAT in the back booth of the Italian restaurant to eat their meal. Even though she'd told him she had eaten Italian food before, it'd only been once when Ada had brought over Italian takeaway when she and *Mamm* were both unwell. It wasn't long after Florence's father had died.

They sat and talked about the life they'd create together while sharing a large bowl of spaghetti Bolognese. He taught her how to use her fork against the bowl of her spoon to twirl a few noodles around the fork for a manageable mouthful. It was messy which resulted in a lot of laughter. After that, they ordered dessert and Carter requested the bill.

As he finished the last of his gelato ice cream, he placed the spoon down on the plate. "Thanks for coming out with me today."

"Thanks for asking me." She looked into his handsome face and felt like she must be the happiest girl in the world. Right at that moment, she felt like no one else existed – not her family, not the Amish community, and definitely not Ezekiel Troyer. She was carefree, like that windblown autumn leaf, and it felt good. If only she could be like that always … just living for the day and taking no care for tomorrow.

"You make me smile," Carter said softly.

"I hope I always will."

"You've certainly changed my life. And I want to change yours for the better. I want you to have everything that you've ever wanted. I know you don't want much, but there will be things you'll get and wonder how you ever did without them."

She giggled. "Like what?"

"Let me see now, how about things like an electric blanket, blender, electric kettle, or maybe a dishwasher?"

"I would love a dishwasher."

"I have one. I've always had one in every place I've lived. Not that I need one. I just throw the cartons in the trash. No need to wash up my take-out containers."

Florence laughed aloud at the pretend-serious way he spoke such silliness, causing him to break into a cheeky grin.

"We're going to have such a good life, you and I," he said, turning fully serious. "We can travel the world if that's what you want. We can see the lions and elephants in Africa, we can go to Pompeii and see the ruins, Egypt to see the pyramids. Whatever you want."

"I've always thought the best part about traveling is coming home again."

"So, you have traveled?"

"When my father was alive, we used to go to other communities for weddings and funerals and such. We'd never go far. Not like going out of the country or anything. I'd rather be home surrounded by my own things."

"And that's ideal for the owner of an orchard, but as my wife, we can pay others to do that. Or, you can manage it and pay someone to step in when we're not there."

It sounded like an ideal life. Almost too good to be true. She hoped nothing came in the way of them marrying. "I guess I'm happy with my own piece of dirt underneath my feet, my own land. That's all I want. If you really want to travel, I'll go with you." She'd be free to do things like that when she left the community.

"We'll see. We'll take what happens when it comes."

"That's always the best way." She spooned the last mouthful of gelato into her mouth. "This meal was so good. Thanks for this."

"You don't have to thank me all the time. We're a couple now."

"I know, but I still like to thank you."

"Thanking is for strangers." He picked up his

napkin, leaned over and wiped her chin, catching a little sauce left over from the Bolognese.

"Oh no! Was that there all the time?" She felt her face flushing with embarrassment.

He laughed. "It's okay, don't be upset. I just noticed it now."

"Are you sure?"

"Positive." He leaned over again but this time it was to give her a quick kiss on the lips. "There. That's how you can thank me in future."

She giggled. "I'll remember that."

"Good. I hope you never forget it."

"Where to now?" she asked.

"Anywhere you want to go."

"I should be getting home soon. We're running low on sugar and I know the girls won't think to get that. Do you mind if we stop by the markets and pick some up?"

"Sugar?"

"Yes. We seem to go through a lot of it."

"Okay, come on. Let's do it." He left the money for the meal and a generous tip on the table and they headed back to the car.

As they walked down the street together, she noticed how the women stared at him and then looked at her. Carter paid no attention to them.

When they got into the car, he looked over at her. "The markets. End of the road, go right, and then left?"

"That's it."

"I don't do much shopping."

"Where do you get your food from?"

"I stock up about once a month. All prepared minute meals that I defrost or microwave directly from the freezer, depending on the directions on the package. It sounds unhealthy but actually some of them are quite good. And then for the rest of the time I live on smoothies made with fruit, protein powder, this and that."

"I can see why you don't need a dishwasher."

"No. I can wash one thing by hand."

"Do the smoothies taste nice?"

"Sometimes yes, sometimes no. Depends what I put in them. I'll make one for you sometime."

"I'd like that." She was pleased she was getting to know more of his daily routine since they'd soon have to work out their new ones together. As he drove to the markets, she asked, "And how much work do you do a day?"

"It varies. Anything from two hours a day to twelve hours a day, depending on what I've got going on. Sometimes I've got troubleshooting, sometimes I've got meetings. It varies widely." He glanced at her. "And that's seven days a week."

She nodded. That meant he worked on Sunday. "We have a day of rest on every Sunday."

"And that's a good idea. I've always thought I'd like to stop for one day and just do nothing. Perhaps I will do that every Sunday with you, and switch off everything."

"Would you?"

"I don't see why not … marriage is a compromise, isn't it? Always thinking what the other person wants?"

"It is."

"And you can't be the only one who's doing the compromising. I'm willing to change my life to accommodate you and I know you've made the biggest step of the both of us. I'll spend the rest of my life making that up to you."

She didn't want it to be like that. All she wanted was for things to be normal between them. "You don't have to do that. It's the decision I've made and I'm happy to do it."

"It's nice to hear you say that."

They pulled into the parking lot of the markets. "Do you know those people over there?"

She looked where he nodded his head. It was a horse and buggy and then … there was Cherish.

Cherish was there talking to a man. "Yes, that's my sister, Cherish, the one who just got back." She looked closer and saw that the man she was talking to was Tom, Larry's employee. "Oh no!"

"What's the matter?"

"She's talking with someone she shouldn't be talking with."

Carter looked over at them. "He looks safe enough

to me."

"He's safe enough, but he's engaged … to someone else. He delivered feed yesterday and I told her to keep away from him. And now, here they are talking."

"I see."

"I'll have to tell her to find her sisters and go home." She opened the car door.

"Do you want me to wait here?"

"Would you?"

"Of course. I'll wait right here."

"Thank you. Her sisters won't be too far." She gave him a quick kiss on the cheek before she got out of the car. She stared at the two offenders. Cherish was acting all coy looking up at Tom, and he had one arm leaning against the buggy and the other hand on his hip. There was no question that they were both attracted to each other. Tom was looking mighty pleased with himself. He should've known better than to encourage her.

"Cherish." When Florence called out, they both jumped apart.

"What are you doing here?" Cherish asked when Florence reached them.

Florence eyed both of them, ignoring her sister's question. "What are *you* doing here, Cherish?"

"I told you I was coming here and you said it was okay."

She certainly hadn't allowed her to come here to talk to Tom. "That's right. Where are the girls now?"

"They went home and left me here by myself. Tom's

offered to drive me home, so you don't need to worry. I'll be safe."

"That's right. I'll take good care of her." Tom smiled, but didn't make eye-contact.

"And how's Isabel, Tom?" Florence asked.

That wiped the smile from his face. "She's fine. She's at work at the moment, doesn't finish until five."

"That's convenient." She looked back at Cherish. "Just as well I turned up then because you can come home with us."

"Us?"

"That's right. Our neighbor's here."

"I'll go, then if you've got a ride home, Cherish," Tom said. He touched his hat. "Nice to see you again, Florence. Goodbye, Cherish. I'll see you soon."

"I'll see you on Sunday, Tom."

He nodded and then backed away.

Florence grabbed her by the arm and marched her back to the car and opened the door. "Carter, is it alright if we take Cherish home?"

"Sure."

"Thanks." She opened the back door and pushed Cherish in.

"Steady," Cherish complained.

"Cherish, is it?" Carter asked, twisting to look at her.

"That's right. And you're the friendly neighbor?"

"It seems so. The name is Carter. Put your seatbelt on."

Florence got into the car and snapped on her belt. "Good, you two have already introduced yourselves."

"We have." He nodded. "I'm guessing we're forgetting about the sugar?" he asked Florence.

"Yes, we'll just have to go without sugar."

"Joy got some," Cherish said.

Florence half twisted to look at Cherish. "She did?"

"Yes."

"*Wunderbaar.*" It was so rare her sisters thought for themselves.

"I wasn't doing anything wrong, Florence. There's nothing wrong with him doing that."

"Doing what?"

"He was just going to drive me home. He was just being nice."

"You have to be careful – he's engaged to another woman. What would happen if other people saw you riding in his buggy and they told Isabel before he told Isabel he drove you home?"

Carter drove out of the parking lot.

After a moment, Cherish said, "It's not my problem."

"It soon would be your problem."

"Which way?" Carter asked.

"Left, then right and then follow that road. Then, I think you'll recognize the way." Florence didn't want to sound too harsh on her younger sister in front of Carter. He wouldn't understand their ways, and what they thought was inappropriate was probably mild to him.

"What do you think, Mr. Carter?"

He chuckled. "It's Carter Braithwaite and I agree with anything Florence says."

"Yeah, well, you would."

His response made Florence very happy. Cherish's did not.

"Anyway, let's just say I was in love with Tom and he was in love with me, then he should end things with Isabel and be with me, isn't that so?"

"I doubt that's the case," Florence said, "so, there's no point discussing it further."

"But supposing that it were," Cherish persisted.

"Well you don't want to marry a man who's got the same name as Aunt Dagmar's annoying bird, do you?"

Cherish giggled. "That's Timmy, Florence. The bird's name is Timmy, not Tom."

"*Ach,* I thought it was Tommy."

"No. You're so funny sometimes, Florence."

When they got closer to home, Carter asked Florence, "Shall we take Cherish home and then you come back with me?"

Florence didn't know what to say. It would look odd to take Cherish home and go back to his place to spend some time. "It's getting a bit late, perhaps—"

"Go back to his place, it's okay. I won't tell anyone."

"It's not like that," Florence said.

"Sure it's not." Cherish giggled. "Your secret's safe with me."

"There are no secrets," Florence blurted out before she remembered that there were, but she wasn't the one keeping them.

When the car stopped, Cherish jumped out. "Thank you, Mr. Carter."

"It's not—" he started, but before he could correct her, she was gone.

"Don't worry about her, she knows what she said. She's just being silly. I'm sorry we have to cut our time short today."

"Don't be. We'll have plenty more time together soon. I'll go home and hang up your new clothes."

"Thank you for all of them, and for such a beautiful day. I had a really good time."

"I'm pleased you came with me, and may we have many, many more." He grabbed her hand and slowly pressed his lips against it sending tingles throughout her whole body.

CHAPTER 10

THAT NIGHT, Florence waited the entire way through dinner hoping *Mamm* would share her news with the girls.

"I miss *Dat* and Mark, and also Earl," said Cherish out of the blue while they ate apple pie and whipped cream for dessert.

"We'll have Mark over for dinner soon," Florence told her.

Isaac smiled. "I'll tell Mark you miss him when I see him at work tomorrow. He might stop by to see you. I don't think he knew you were coming home so soon."

"*Denke*, Isaac. I also miss Aunt Dagmar. It's kind of boring without her. She's nice when you get to know her. Caramel likes her dogs, but he doesn't run around with them like he does with Goldie."

"What about Tom?" Florence heard Hope whisper to Cherish.

Cherish quickly dug her in the ribs. "Shh."

"Who's Tom?" *Mamm* asked.

"Isabel's Tom," Joy said.

Mamm stared at Cherish. "What have you done now, Cherish?"

"I haven't done anything. Why?" Cherish leaned forward. "What have you heard?"

"I heard Hope say something about Tom just now."

"Don't worry about her, she doesn't know what she's talking about."

At that moment, the two dogs ran through the kitchen and under the table, threaded their way between all of their legs and then out the other side. "Will someone get up and open the front door so those dogs can play outside?" *Mamm* muttered.

When no one volunteered, Florence stood up. "I'll do it." She chased the dogs out the front door and then closed it after them, wishing she had half their energy. To Florence's surprise she saw buggy lights heading to the house. She hoped it might be Mark coming to see Cherish. Then she saw that it was the bishop. It was most unusual to get a visit from Bishop Paul.

"It's the bishop," she called out. "With someone else. I can't quite see who it is. It's a man." When they got closer, the face became clearer. "It's Eli Morgan." Eli was a deacon. She saw their faces looked quite somber and she wondered what had happened.

Had somebody died?

When the two men got out of the buggy, Florence met them halfway from the house in case she had to deliver bad news to *Mamm*. She might be able to do it in a more gentle manner.

"What is it, Bishop Paul? Is something wrong?"

He adjusted his thick glasses. "I'm here to talk to Wilma about her youngest *dochder*."

"Cherish?"

"That's right."

"She only just got here yesterday."

He didn't answer, he just stared at her, waiting. "Come in, I'll get *Mamm*."

She went into the house and her mother was coming out of the kitchen. "It's the bishop?"

"*Jah*, and Eli Morgan."

"What do they want?"

She looked over *Mamm's* shoulder at the girls still at the kitchen table. "They want to talk to you about Cherish, that's what they said."

"What have you done?" *Mamm* asked Cherish.

"Nothing. Nothing at all. Unless …. Unless someone is telling lies about me."

"I'll wait in here with the girls, *Mamm*."

"*Nee*, can you come with me, Florence?"

"Sure." *Mamm* closed the door of the kitchen so the girls wouldn't hear, and then headed to talk to the bishop and Eli in the living room. Florence followed.

After they greeted Wilma, they all sat down.

"Can I make either of you tea or coffee?" Wilma asked.

"Nee." They both shook their heads.

"Cherish was seen out in the early hours of the morning with Tom Beckett."

Mamm drew her eyebrows together. "No, it's not possible. She was here last night."

Florence looked over at her mother. Didn't she realize that Cherish had sneaked out of the house?

"She might have got back before you woke, Wilma."

Florence could see Wilma's agitation by the way her hands were clasped in her lap. "Did you see her with your own eyes?" Wilma asked.

"I didn't," the bishop replied.

"What makes you think it was Cherish? Somebody might have mistakenly seen someone else and thought it was Cherish. Especially if it was night time. Who is accusing her?"

"I am. I saw her with my own eyes," Eli Morgan said. "I was out late consoling a couple who had just been delivered tragic news and I was traveling home at a little before two in the morning. I saw the both of them."

Mamm's fingers flew to her mouth and she sat there not knowing what to say, so Florence knew she would have to take over. "We will talk to her and she will be punished. You don't have to be concerned about that. We'll keep a closer eye on her."

"I appreciate that, Florence, but this is something for the elders."

The bishop continued, "I will talk to both of them separately and see what each of them has to say, and the elders will decide what to do with them."

Florence nodded. There was no arguing with the bishop and the elders.

"Do you want to talk to her now?" Wilma asked.

"We are gathering the elders at my *haus* at four tomorrow afternoon. Bring Cherish then."

"*Jah*, we will," said *Mamm*.

"Good."

Florence then showed the bishop and Eli out of the house while *Mamm* stayed seated. As soon as Florence got back into the house, she saw that the girls were gathered around *Mamm* and she'd told them everything.

Cherish's face had completely drained of color and Florence almost felt sorry for her.

Cherish looked up at Florence. "What will I do?"

"Just go and see what they have to say. Admit your wrongdoing and accept their punishment."

"I didn't do anything wrong."

"We'll figure something out," said *Mamm*.

Florence was disappointed about what had happened. Now *Mamm* wouldn't tell them about Carter, not tonight. "There's nothing to figure out. She'll be punished. No one else can help her."

Cherish burst into tears and ran up the stairs.

"See what you've done now, Florence? You could show more compassion," *Mamm* said.

Florence put her fists on her hips. "Cherish should've thought of this before she sneaked out of the *haus*."

"How is this now Florence's fault?" asked Joy. "Cherish is spoiled and she should learn her lesson, and it's about time. She's always been spoilt and she thinks she can do anything."

Favor shook her head. "She's only young. Give her time. There's no need for people to be mean."

THERE WAS SO much chatter going on in the house, and Cherish's loud sobs were coming from upstairs. All of the racket made Florence's head hurt. She left them all and walked out into the cool evening, closing the front door behind her. *Mamm,* Favor and Cherish all thought she was mean. Well, maybe they were right, but it was no good being soft on a child, and Cherish was still young – and behaving like a child.

At last, some peace. She took a couple of deep breaths of air to calm her nerves, and shrugged off the opinions of others. It wasn't pleasant for Cherish to have to go in front of the elders, but she had to learn she couldn't do certain things.

As she was trying – and failing – to find a place in her heart that felt sorry for Cherish, she heard the phone in the barn start ringing.

When it rang late at night, it meant an emergency. She hurried to the barn, opened the door and then grabbed the flashlight. As she flicked it on, she was already making her way to the phone, hurrying to reach it before it stopped. Grabbing the phone's receiver, she held it up to her ear. "Hello?"

"Have I got the Bakers?"

"Yes, this is Florence. Who's this?" It wasn't a voice she recognized.

"This is a friend and neighbor of Dagmar Baker's."

Her heart sank. Florence knew something bad had happened to Dagmar.

"She wanted me to call. She gave me this number. She's not very well."

Florence let out the breath she'd been holding onto. If she wasn't 'very well,' that meant she was alive, at least. "What's wrong with her?"

"She had a fall and broke her leg. She should be home from the hospital tomorrow morning."

"Oh, that's dreadful. Thank you for letting me know. Who is this, please?"

"Oh, I'm sorry, this is Rita. I'm a neighbor of hers. Are you Cherish's mother?"

"I'm Cherish's sister."

"Would you make sure you let Cherish know?"

"I will. I certainly will. And what is your phone number if I might have that?"

Florence moved forward and grabbed the pen that they kept near the phone and jotted down the number.

"Thank you. Does Dagmar have anybody to look after her?"

"There are people in her community helping her."

"You're not a member of the community?"

"No. I called in to see if she was okay and found her lying there, unable to move. A voice in my head had told me to visit her. Just as well."

"Thank you. I'm grateful you did."

"I know Cherish well. I was sad to hear she left to go home."

"I didn't know Cherish knew too many people."

"She does. She gets about."

"Thank you, Rita. I'll be sure to let Cherish know, and our mother. Please call me if we can do anything at all to help."

"Thank you, Florence."

There was a loud click and then Florence replaced the receiver.

She walked back to the house, opened the front door, and Cherish was standing there staring at her with red-rimmed eyes.

"Was that the phone I heard?" Cherish asked.

"Yes, it was."

"Has someone said I've done something else?"

There was more? Florence didn't want to know. *"Nee,* it was someone telling me about Aunt Dagmar."

"What's wrong with her?"

"She's had a fall and broken her leg."

"Ach nee, that's terrible. I bet she slipped on those

stupid tiles out the back door. They're slippery when it rains. Who's looking after her?"

"The woman on the phone said that the community is looking after her when she gets out of the hospital tomorrow morning."

"Nobody in the community would be able to look after her and give her three meals a day and feed all the animals. They all live too far away. The bishop lives fairly close, but he and his wife are so busy."

Florence shrugged her shoulders. "Maybe the neighbors are helping. She said she was Rita."

"*Nee*, Rita's old. Poor Aunt Dagmar will starve to death and get eaten by her cats. I need to go back and be with her." She left Florence and ran to her mother. "Maybe I should go and see how she is, *Mamm*."

Florence walked over to everyone who'd been listening in. "Maybe I should go."

Cherish shook her head. "No, you don't know what to do and you won't be able to feed all the animals."

"Of course I do. I was raised on a farm with lots of animals."

"No, you won't be able to keep up with the workload. It's not easy, you know."

Mamm said, "If she gets out of the hospital tomorrow, how about I organize a car to take you back tomorrow?"

Cherish's bottom lip quivered and her eyes filled with tears, for the second time that night.

Florence was sure the second bout of tears were

genuine. She was close to Dagmar. Florence stepped forward and hugged her. "It'll be alright. She'll be okay."

"*Jah, Mamm,* I need to go back there. She might have been lying there for days, or hours anyway, with a broken leg. She lives so far away from anyone, she could've died and nobody would've found her."

"It's okay. They did find her and she's perfectly okay. And you'll go back there and look after her and everything will be just fine."

"What if I can't get a driver?" Cherish sobbed.

"Florence, organize her a car, would you?"

"Okay, but should we call the bishop first and—?"

"*Nee,*" Mamm cut across her. "This is an emergency. A family emergency."

Cherish sniffed. "*Denke,* Florence."

"What about going to the bishop's tomorrow, *Mamm?* Remember you were going with Cherish at four?"

"This is an emergency, Florence. He'll understand."

"Okay, if you think so. I just take the orders around here, it seems." Florence headed back to the barn pleased that she was seeing a softer and more mature side of Cherish. It must've been the right thing to send Cherish to Dagmar's. She was glad, though, that she wasn't going to be the one telling the bishop about Cherish leaving suddenly.

. . .

AFTER FLORENCE WAS able to organize a driver and car, she headed back into the house. "I've got a car coming at six, Cherish."

"*Denke,* Florence. I was hoping to leave earlier than that, but it'll have to do."

"Six in the morning, I meant," Florence told her.

"Ah. *Denke.* That's perfect."

WHEN THE GIRLS went to bed that night, Wilma and Florence sat together sewing. Florence was still disappointed that Wilma hadn't told the girls that Carter was their cousin, but she begrudgingly admitted that it was understandable given the emergency.

"Would you go to the bishop tomorrow and explain the situation? Tell him about Aunt Dagmar, and Cherish going back to look after her."

Florence gulped. She wouldn't have been so pleased for Cherish to go if she'd known that was going to be expected of her. "Me?"

Mamm nodded.

"Isn't that your job as the head of the household?"

"I haven't been feeling well. I would've hoped you'd want to do something small like that for me." *Mamm* lowered her needlework and stared at Florence.

Small? Since when was delivering upsetting news to the bishop something small? "He won't be happy that Cherish avoided her punishment, or lecture, or whatever discipline he had planned for her." Florence sighed. "Okay, I'll do it. I'll go at four and tell him—"

"*Nee,* go first thing in the morning, so he doesn't waste any more time."

"Okay. Good thinking, I suppose. I'll go after breakfast, and as soon as Cherish has gone."

CHAPTER 11

IN THE MORNING, everybody was in tears because Cherish was going – everyone, that was, except for Florence. Cherish had brought trouble with her whenever she'd been home since sending her to Dagmar's. Dagmar seemed to have no problem with her and she needed help on the farm. It was an ideal situation for everyone.

When the car pulled up, Cherish hugged everyone goodbye.

The driver walked forward and picked up a suitcase from her. "Is this it?"

"That's all I've got."

She walked over to the car and called her dog, but he wouldn't come. "Caramel, come," Cherish demanded for a third time. "He's too busy playing with Goldie. He'll have more fun here with Goldie than he'll have with Dagmar's old dogs. I feel it'd be cruel taking him with me. Will you look after him if I leave him, Joy? I'll be back as soon as Aunt Dagmar gets better."

"Of course I will. I'll take the very best care of him, as though he was my own dog."

Mamm said, "Are you sure you want to leave him?"

"It might be better that way. I'll have so much more work to do if she's bedridden. I'll have to do all her work and all the work I used to do for her as well."

It sounded like Cherish was getting used to doing hard work, but in her own home, she was the same lazy Cherish who'd left.

"Off you go then if you think you can live without Caramel for a few weeks," *Mamm* said in response to Cherish standing there staring after the dogs as they ran about the yard.

"I will if Joy looks after him."

"Of course. I already said I would."

Cherish got into the car and the driver closed the trunk. A few minutes later, she was gone.

Mamm cried into a handkerchief. "It's hard seeing her come back and I'm so joyful, and then she goes and I'm so sad again." Joy put her arm around her mother.

"She's doing charitable works looking after Dagmar when she's laid up."

"I know, but still, she is my youngest." She then looked up at Florence. "Don't forget you've got to see the bishop today."

"I won't forget. It's hard to forget something like that." Florence shuddered. "I still haven't figured out what I'm going to say. He might think we've sent her away so she could avoid getting punished."

"He wouldn't," Favor said.

"It seems a good excuse though, a good excuse for us to send her away before she could get into trouble," Joy agreed.

"I don't think she would've gotten into that much trouble, though," Hope said. "She was probably just going to get a stern warning."

Slowly, Florence nodded. "And now she's been spared from that stern warning."

"It's not your fault," Joy said to Florence.

"Let's just hope the bishop sees it that way."

Everyone walked back inside the house. As always, everything had been dumped on Florence's shoulders. Gone was the carefree girl of yesterday who was giggling, trying on clothes, and eating Italian food.

ON HER WAY to the bishop's house, she stopped by Carter's. He would give her strength to face the bishop. Although, she didn't feel like telling him what she had to see the bishop about. He would think it was ridiculous for people to have to explain themselves in that way, but Cherish was so young. Maybe he'd understand.

She could see when she turned her buggy into his driveway that he wasn't home. She didn't know where he could be at that hour of the morning since he was usually home all day.

Then when she got level with the house to turn the buggy around, she saw a car. It belonged to the woman who worked for him, she was sure about that. She'd seen that car before on a couple of occasions.

She figured they were out somewhere having a business meeting over breakfast. As she pointed the buggy back towards the road, she wondered exactly what job the woman did. And also, why did they need to have their meetings in person rather than over the phone?

Florence prayed all the way to Bishop Paul's house. The first thing was, she hoped he'd be home because she didn't want to turn around and come back again later. It would only add to her nervousness. The second thing was, she hoped he'd understand that Cherish needed to look after their aunt.

WHEN FLORENCE ARRIVED at the bishop's house, she hurried to the front door and knocked on it, hoping to get her visit over as soon as possible. Then she'd get back home and find out from Wilma when she'd be telling the news about Carter to the girls.

"Florence! Come in. How nice to see you."

"You too, Mary. Is Bishop Paul home?"

"*Jah*, he is. He's just finished breakfast. Would you like a cup of *kaffe*?"

"*Nee, denke*, I'm fine. I've just had one at home."

As Florence stepped through the doorway, Mary said, "Isn't Wilma coming to see him this evening?"

"Well, not anymore. That's what I've come to see him about."

"Well, no good telling me because you'd have to tell it all to my husband again."

When they walked into the kitchen, she saw the bishop sitting there with one of their grandchildren.

"*Gut mayrie,* Florence. What can I do for you on this beautiful day *Gott* has given us? Sit down."

She gave a little giggle to ease her nerves somewhat, and sat down while Mary continued her work in the kitchen. Florence had taken little time to think about the weather or if it was a nice day or not. "You're expecting Cherish and my mother here later today, but there was an emergency." She hoped he would see it as an emergency.

"Go on."

"My Aunt Dagmar, *Dat's schweschder,* has broken her leg and she has no one to work the farm, or to look after her. Cherish had to go back there early this morning."

"I see … and when did all this happen?" As he spoke the motion of his jaws wiggled his bushy gray beard.

"Last night we got the call that she had been injured. It was after you and Eli left. We didn't want to trouble you when we found out. It was very late." Florence wasn't pleased she had to be the one sitting in front of the bishop. It was something *Mamm* should've done, or Cherish could've spoken to him herself and told him she was leaving. They'd both placed her in an awkward position. "Cherish left this morning. I didn't call you because I thought it was best to speak to you in person today."

"Very well. *Denke* for stopping by and letting me know. She won't escape this. I'll talk to her when she returns."

Florence nodded. "I'm not sure when that will be. It depends solely on Dagmar."

Finally, his face relaxed into a smile. "*Jah*, of course it does. That gives me some free time this afternoon after we talk to Tom."

Florence was more than slightly relieved when he relaxed.

"Are you sure you don't want to have a cup of tea or coffee?" Mary asked, poking her head in from the kitchen.

"I might have a cup of *kaffe, denke.*"

She felt a little odd sitting there in the bishop's house knowing that she was going to leave the community and marry Carter, but she couldn't tell him, not yet. She'd tell the bishop when everything was arranged. A part of her was holding out, she realized, still hoping Carter would join them.

She stared down at the wooden table wondering if she could speed up Wilma, or should she tell the girls herself that their cousin was living next door? Then they'd have to know all about Iris, but it really wasn't Florence's problem.

"How is the orchard doing, Florence?"

"Quite well, *denke*." The apple orchard was another issue that needed to be sorted before she married Carter. There was so many things to do. When the bishop kept staring at her, she knew that she needed to make some conversation. "And how have you been?"

He slurped a mouthful of coffee, and then said, "As busy as ever."

"I hear Joy and Isaac are looking to get married," Mary said as she placed a mug of coffee in front of Florence.

"*Denke*." She looked up at Mary. "That won't be for quite some time."

"The end of the year," the bishop said.

Florence's eyebrows shot up. "Really?"

"*Jah*, they both came to see me about getting baptized."

"Oh. That's something they didn't tell me."

"It seems sometimes family is often last to know these things."

She nodded. "It seems so." Now she had to stay and drink the largest mug of coffee she'd ever seen, when she'd only just had two cups at home. While she was doing that, she had to talk. "How's *schul*, Michael?" she asked the bishop's grandson, guessing he would've been about twelve. He must've been used to hearing snippets of things when he was staying at his grandparents' house.

"Yeah, well, it's alright. Can't wait until I don't have to go anymore."

Florence giggled. "Enjoy it while you can. When you leave your life will be full of chores."

"I'd rather that than learning things I'll never need to know."

"I'm sure everything they're teaching you will come in handy. I never thought I'd need math and now I use it every day because of the orchard. When you grow up and have your own *haus* and a business of sorts, you'll need it too."

"That's what they tell me." He rolled his eyes. "I still don't like it. I'd rather be outdoors, farming, helping *Dat* plow."

"Me too. I love being outdoors." The conversation flowed a little easier when Mary sat down with them. Not long after she did, the bishop left with his grandson.

Florence stared into her cup. There was still two thirds of it to go. She took a large mouthful, swallowing it like medicine now that it was a little cooler.

"Is everything else all right, Florence?"

"*Jah*, it is." Had Mary heard something about Carter already? If Mary knew, she clearly hadn't said anything to her husband. "Why do you ask?"

"You look a little worried or upset about something."

Florence giggled, to make what she was about to say more believable. "Nothing more than usual. It was worrying to hear the news of Dagmar, and we thought Cherish was home for good, but then she insisted on being there for Dagmar. She's turning into such a thoughtful girl. From what I've heard, Dagmar has many animals and it's tough work for one person, and impossible when that person has a broken leg, or foot. I'm not sure which. I just know that she's off her feet."

"Florence, I've been meaning to ask you to join our ladies group."

That was something Florence hadn't wanted to do. All of the ladies were married and had children, and she'd have been the odd one out. She preferred to stay home rather than go to gatherings like that. And now there'd be no point, but she'd best act a little curious. "Which one?"

"The new one that we're starting up. We meet once a week to coordinate helping the unfortunate with our charitable deeds."

"I would, but with the orchard, I'm left little time for anything."

"I can understand that. What about Wilma?"

"She'd love to join, I'm sure." Florence laughed inside. That would teach Wilma. Next time, she might do her own unpleasant tasks. *"Jah,* I'm sure she'd like that."

"Gut. I'll talk to her about it at the next meeting."

Florence nodded, knowing her stepmother hadn't

joined any of the other ladies' meetings. Wilma helped out where she could, but she didn't like going to any more meetings than need be. After another large gulp of coffee, she looked into the mug pleased she only had a third to go.

"You don't have to drink it all," Mary said.

"Oh, that's good. I had a lot of coffee at home, and I've had enough now."

"When did Cherish leave?"

"This morning."

"I hope Dagmar will be okay."

Florence smiled. "I'm sure she will be now. She'll be so happy to see Cherish back there to help her. I should go. *Denke* for the *kaffe.*" Florence stood, and Mary walked her out of the house.

WHEN FLORENCE DROVE AWAY from the bishop's house, she let out a loud sigh of relief. Then her thoughts turned to her mother. It had been a surprise to learn her mother had been an outsider and had joined the Amish before she married *Dat*. Ada had been the one to tell her that, and she still hadn't discussed it with Wilma or anyone else. She was certain that her two brothers didn't know that either. Maybe that was why no one ever talked about their mother – because no one really knew her.

CHAPTER 12

THE CAR BROUGHT Cherish up the driveway and stopped in front of Dagmar's farmhouse. "Thank you – you've been paid, right?"

"That's right."

"Good." She didn't have much money with her. She only had the money that she had kept from selling baskets the last time she went to the markets with Aunt Dagmar, and the markets were only held once a month in their part of the world.

"Thank you." She got out and started walking to the house, feeling sad about Caramel staying behind. Maybe that had been the wrong decision.

"Miss!"

She turned around.

"I have to get your bag out of the trunk."

"Ah, that's right."

"I'll bring it in for you." He lifted the trunk and brought out the bag.

"I'll take it." She walked over and grabbed her suitcase from him. "Thanks again."

"No problem."

As she walked to the farmhouse, she heard the car door shut and the car's engine start. By the time she got to the door the car was at the bottom of the driveway. The front door was unlocked, so she pulled it open and called out. "Aunt Dagmar?"

"Cherish? Cherish is that you?" The tiny voice came from the bedroom.

"*Jah,* it's me." Cherish dumped her bag just inside the door and opened the bedroom door to see Aunt Dagmar lying in bed with her foot in a plaster cast that went all the way to her knee. That leg was raised on a fat pillow. She rushed to her side. "Aunt Dagmar, are you okay?" When Dagmar smiled, she reminded Cherish so much of her father.

"I'm okay."

Cherish moved the quilt to one side and sat down on the side of her aunt's bed. "How did this happen?"

Dagmar gave a gruff sound from the back of her throat as though she was irritated with herself. "I was hurrying down the stairs when it was raining, and the stairs moved."

"What do you mean, 'the stairs moved?'"

Aunt Dagmar's lips twitched at the corners. "They

moved, they weren't where they were supposed to be and that's why I tripped."

Cherish giggled. Not only did Aunt Dagmar look like her father, they shared the same sense of humor. "You've got to be more careful in the rain. I told you it's all slippery out there."

"I'm always careful."

"You weren't when this happened."

"You didn't need to come back all this way to tell me that."

She patted Dagmar's arm. "I had to come back to look after you."

"I can look after myself, but I'm glad you came back."

"You mean if I hadn't come back, nobody would be looking after you?"

"The Shetlers are checking on me."

She shook her head. "That's not good enough. Rita's old. You need someone staying here with you, looking after you, and that's why I'm here."

"You're a dear girl. Did you leave your family and your friends just to come back and look after me?"

"Not only that, I missed you and the farm."

That made Aunt Dagmar smile. "Where's Caramel?"

"I left him behind."

"Why?"

"Joy has got a new puppy and they love playing

together. They play from sunup to sundown and I thought it would be easier if I left Caramel there."

"I see."

"Can I get you anything?"

"Rita brought me some soup. It just needs heating."

"Oh good. Do you want some of it now?"

"Yes, please. They put enough feed out for the animals too. They're due back day after tomorrow – the Shetlers are."

Cherish was horrified that Dagmar would have been here by herself for so long. Just as well she'd come back. The Shetlers were the closest neighbors, an older couple in their eighties. "I don't know how the community thought you would manage here by yourself for that long. What about the animals? They have to be fed, the cows and goats have to be milked."

"I wasn't worried. *Gott* always makes a way. You came back, you see?" Dagmar's thin mouth curved into a smile, making Cherish giggle once more.

"That's right I did." At that moment, she was reminded of Joy who would've quoted half a dozen Scriptures by now about how the Lord provided. She didn't mind knowing what God's word said, she just didn't like Joy quoting it at every opportunity. "I'll heat up that soup and while I'm doing that I'll check on the animals and see what they need." She knew she'd have to milk those animals she'd just mentioned.

"*Denke*, Cherish. You're a *gut* girl. I'm so glad you've come back. I've gotten used to your company."

"And I missed you when I left." Cherish leaned over Dagmar and kissed her forehead, pushing away strands of unruly gray hair as she did so. "When you're finished eating, I'll brush your hair and I'll braid it."

Still smiling, Dagmar closed her eyes.

Cherish hurried out of the room. No one had ever said that they liked having her around. She always felt like such a nuisance. None of her sisters really liked her because they were always calling her spoiled. But if she was spoiled and favored by *Mamm*, her mother wouldn't have been so quick to send her away – not once, but twice.

She found the soup, which appeared to be a mixture of corn and vegetables and a small amount of chicken, and she poured it into a saucepan and placed it over a low flame. While the soup heated, she headed out to check on the animals.

The chickens were without food and were staring at her looking hungry. The three milking cows bellowed when they saw her and the goats were calling, too. Just as well she'd put the soup on a low flame.

After the milking was finished, she fed all the animals and topped off their water. Then she checked on the two horses. They both shared a stable off from the yard. When she approached, they walked over for a pat.

Remembering the soup, she ran back to the house. It had steam rising from it and that told her it had heated through. She quickly washed her hands in the mud room after she changed into the clean shoes that she'd left behind. She ladled out a dish of soup and placed it on a tray with some bread she'd found.

When she got back into Aunt Dagmar's room, her aunt was fast asleep. She put the tray on the nightstand and for some reason, she looked to see if her aunt was breathing since she was lying there so still. When she could see no sign of life, she moved closer to see if she could feel breath coming out of her nose. "Aunt Dagmar!" She shook her shoulder and stared at her. Then Aunt Dagmar's head rolled to one side. "Aunt Dagmar!" she screamed.

She was dead.

Cherish stared at her aunt and shook her again, still trying to wake her. "Aunt Dagmar." She took a couple of steps back wondering what to do.

Florence would know.

She ran to the barn and called home. No one answered, so she dialed again and prayed hard. After the second ring, Florence answered.

"Florence, it's me."

"What's wrong?"

"Aunt Dagmar's dead!"

"What?"

"She was alive when I got here. I heated soup for her, and when I finished … she was dead." There was silence on the other end of the line. "I shouldn't have gone out to check the animals. I should've gone back to see if she was okay. I was heating up the soup and while that was happening I checked the animals. The cows were bellowing, I had to milk them. Why did I do that Florence? Why didn't I stay with her? She might not have died if I did that."

"The Lord was calling her home. There was nothing you could've done."

"What do I do now? Who do I call? I don't know what to do. I'm all alone."

"I'll come as soon as I can. I'll call Dagmar's bishop. He'll know what to do."

"Do you have his number?"

"I do. It's in the address book here somewhere. I'll find it. Don't panic, Cherish. I'll be there as soon as I can."

"*Denke,* Florence. I'm here by myself." Cherish sobbed.

"I'll be there. You'll be okay. Just sit down, calm down, and have something to eat."

"The soup. I left soup on the stove."

"Quick, go see to the soup and I'll get ready to go."

Cherish hung up the receiver and walked back into the house with tears flooding down her cheeks. It reminded her of when Dat had died. It too had been sudden. After she turned off the stove, she went back into Dagmar's room and covered her with a sheet. Then she moved the sheet to give her a quick kiss on her forehead.

"I love you, Dagmar. I wish I had told you that." She wiped tears from her eyes. "I hope you can hear that now from wherever you are. I don't know if you're looking down on me right now, but I wish you hadn't died. It was fun here with you and I am glad it was just you and me, away from my sisters. I'll be a much better person so I don't disappoint you. I'll remember all the things you taught me."

She decided then and there to stay on until everything was settled. The animals would have to find new owners, ones who would treat them right, and most likely, all of Dagmar's things would have to be sold. Having no children of her own, Cherish and her siblings were the closest relatives she had.

CHAPTER 13

FLORENCE ENDED the call from Cherish. Her stomach burned with trepidation as she lifted her hand to her face and bit lightly into her knuckles. There were so many things to do, so many things to organize.

She found the number of Bishop Zachariah from Dagmar's community and told him what had happened and that Cherish had returned and was there by herself.

Then she walked to the house to break the news to her mother and her sisters.

"Who was on the phone?" *Mamm* asked.

There was no other way to say it but to just say it straight out. "It was Cherish. She called to tell me that Aunt Dagmar has died." Everyone sat there looking at her in shock. "It's true." She sat down with them. "I told Cherish I'd go there right away."

Mamm nodded. "*Denke,* Florence."

"I'll have Carter drive me, if he can."

"Poor Cherish. That would be such a shock for her. I'll go with you," Joy said.

"*Nee*. You stay here and look after the dogs."

Favor started crying and Hope comforted her. "It's all right. You barely knew her."

"She was all alone. I hope she didn't die alone. Did she, Florence?"

"Um, I'm not sure. *Nee*, she didn't. Cherish was there. I better go get ready."

"Order a driver," *Mamm* said. "I don't want you driving anywhere with the man next door."

Everyone looked at *Mamm*.

"But didn't she go with him to fetch Honor that time?" Joy asked.

"That was an emergency," *Mamm* snapped.

"*Mamm*, can I talk with you alone?"

She shrugged her shoulders. "Okay."

"Let's go into the living room."

Once she was sitting alone with Wilma, she knew she had to talk quickly. "*Mamm*, I was being patient with you, but with Cherish's news, I've run out of patience. I'm leaving the community to marry Carter and I'm not going to change my mind."

Mamm gasped and stared at her. "I know you said that, but surely you can't be serious?"

"*Jah*, I am. So, by the time I get back, I want you to have told the girls that he's their cousin, okay?"

Mamm shook her head. "You're making a huge mistake. Your *vadder* wouldn't want you to do that."

"Maybe my *mudder* would. Anyway, I have to do what's right for me."

"It's a bad example to the girls."

"As I'm constantly reminded, I'm not the girls' *mudder,* you are. I've spent my whole life looking after everyone else and worrying about other people. I have an opportunity for love and for a family. I'm not letting it pass by. If you don't tell them who Carter is, it'll be left to me. Like everything else around here is left to me."

"We'll talk when you get back."

"I'll grab a few things." Florence raced up the stairs, taking them two at a time. She dragged her suit-case off the top of the free-standing wardrobe, flipped it open, and threw in the things she needed. Then she headed downstairs and saw the girls lined up at the door.

"*Denke,* Florence." Joy ran to her and hugged her. "I don't know what we'd ever do without you."

A pang of guilt ran through Florence. They'd be doing without her soon.

When Joy stepped back, the other girls hugged her in turn. When they'd finished, Wilma was nowhere to be seen. "Where's *Mamm?*"

The girls looked around, and Joy said, "She was here a moment ago."

"Here I am." She walked downstairs with a coat in her hands and then she handed it to Florence. "Take this. It's the warmest I have. It's thicker than yours.

And we'll talk about that other thing when you get back."

Florence smiled at the kind gesture. "Bye, *Mamm*." She leaned forward and hugged her. "*Denke* for the coat."

Florence hurried out of the house hoping Carter was home. If not, she'd have to try to get a driver. She could imagine what panic Cherish would be feeling. She was the youngest of all the girls and it was awful that she was alone in a house with her aunt's lifeless body. If only they hadn't sent her back to care for Dagmar. Surely someone else could've cared for her.

WHEN FLORENCE REACHED THE FENCE, she saw another car at Carter's place. It was the woman's car again and then she saw Carter and the woman he worked with coming out of the house and heading for Carter's car. She waved, hoping he would look over, but he didn't. Even if she ran, she'd never get to the car before it drove away. She slipped through the fence and started moving as quickly as she could with her suitcase in hand, but the car moved away.

"God, what am I to do now?" She turned around and started walking back home. She'd have to call their usual driver and hope he was free. Then she took another look back at Carter's car, and to her surprise, it was coming back. Had he seen her? He stopped the car and got out and he hurried toward her.

"What's wrong?"

"It's Cherish. She's gone back to Aunt Dagmar's and she just called to say Dagmar has died. She's there by herself and she's so upset.

His gaze dropped to her suitcase. "You want me to take you to her?"

"Yes, if you could. If it's not too much trouble."

He rubbed his chin. "I had a meeting, but I'll shuffle a few things around."

"Are you sure you can do that?"

"Of course. How far away is it again?"

"It'd only be a couple of hours by car. I've got the address."

"Phew. It's not as far as Wisconsin."

She shook her head, too distraught to muster a giggle. "Not as far."

"I'll tell my colleague what's going on."

"Should I wait here?"

"No, come and meet her." He took hold of the suitcase, put a hand on her elbow and guided her to his car. Before they got there, the woman got out and looked at them.

"Maggie, this is Florence."

"Nice to meet you, Florence."

"And you too." Florence admired how nice the woman looked. She was always dressed in slim-fitting tailored clothing and her make-up was subtle, but noticeable at the same time.

"An emergency has come up and I have to drive Florence somewhere. I'll be gone all day."

"And, the meeting?"

"It won't be happening today. Make my excuses, reschedule, and I'll be in touch."

She nodded, and didn't look pleased. She bent down and took her handbag out of the car.

"Emergencies happen," he said as he clicked the button to open the trunk.

The woman walked toward her car and called over her shoulder. "Nice to meet you, Florence."

"And you, Maggie."

They got into the car and zoomed away before Maggie had reached her car.

"She didn't seem pleased," Florence said. "I'm sorry."

"We can't worry about that. These sisters of yours seem to give you a bit of trouble."

"I know. They do."

"Left or right?" he asked when they got to the T intersection.

"Left." She read out the address and he programmed it into his GPS.

"I hope you don't mind that I didn't tell Maggie who you were to me. I would've if she was someone important, but she's just a colleague."

She glanced over at him. "I'm in too much of a panic to notice."

"It's just that with you and your Amish clothes it

would've caused a lot of questions. I don't want people to think I plucked you from the Amish. Although, I guess she'll know that now, won't she?"

"I guess so. I'm sorry about your meeting."

"Hey, you come first. Family and friends come before work, where possible, and I'm at a stage now where I don't have to work every day to put food on the table."

"Yes, you've told me that."

"I guess you're no closer to finding out about the orchard? I know you want to keep that when you leave."

She shook her head. "Wilma and I haven't had a proper talk about anything. Cherish came home and then Dagmar got hurt, then Cherish went back there and now Dagmar's dead. There has been a fair bit going on." She left out the part about Cherish sneaking off in the middle of the night and being in trouble with the bishop. That was a story for another day. "I'm so pleased I caught you before you left."

"I was driving off, and happened to suddenly see you in the rearview mirror. You looked so alone and so upset, I just knew there was something wrong."

"I've never heard Cherish so upset. She's always so carefree. I don't even know if she's ever seen anyone dead before that wasn't in a coffin. Not even our father. It must've given her such a fright."

He reached out and took hold of her hand and returned her smile. "You're a caring person, Florence."

"I have to look after them."

"One day, you'll have to let them go. One day soon. They'll all have to get by without you."

She stared out the window at the fields they passed. What he said was right, but could they get along without her?

WHEN CARTER PULLED up at Dagmar's house, he said, "Do you want me to go?"

She saw two buggies. "It might be best, so I don't have to explain who you are."

"I understand. It's too early. There's one thing I want to say to you before you go. First, I'll get your suitcase." He jumped out of the car and pulled her beat-up old brown suitcase out of the trunk.

She was anxious to comfort her sister and glanced over at the house and then looked back at him.

"Florence, before you came into my life I had no one to care for but myself. To put it a different way, I didn't care about anyone and I didn't know what was missing in my life."

"I know how you feel and it makes me … I don't know how to explain it. It makes me feel safe."

He smiled at her and then tipped his head toward the house. "You better go to her." She put her hand back on the door. "Just don't go meeting any more pig farmers."

"I certainly won't." Florence giggled, and he pulled

her toward him. "Don't forget to call me. I take it there's a phone here somewhere?"

"In the barn and it was only installed recently. Bye, Carter." She took a step away from him, and after one last look into the depth of his eyes, she picked up her suitcase and turned toward the house. By the time she reached the house, he was gone and with it, he took a little piece of her.

CHAPTER 14

CHERISH CHARGED out of the house and nearly knocked her off her feet. "Florence, I'm so glad you're here. I'm so upset." She sobbed on Florence's shoulder and Florence dropped her suitcase.

"The funeral director came and took her body. Her funeral will be Tuesday, the bishop said, and he said he'd have the viewing at his house." Rain began to fall. And they both looked up at the sky. "It's been raining all day. It only just stopped and now it's starting again," Cherish said.

"That's good of him," Florence said of the bishop.

"I know. She left me her farm. Her whole farm. It was in her will."

"Oh, really?" The news caught Florence off guard and despite the rain, she stayed put.

Cherish nodded.

"That was generous." Florence hadn't given thought

to what would become of her aunt's farm, but now she wondered why the farm hadn't been left to all the girls equally. The other girls would say Cherish was definitely the favorite now, at least she was Aunt Dagmar's favorite.

"The bishop told me it was in her will. She gave him a copy just last month. Can you believe it?"

"Nee I can't. How are you?"

"Awful. I feel so sad. I can't believe she's gone, just like that. I was talking to her one minute and she asked for soup. While it was heating, I went to check on the animals. If I hadn't done that … I should've gone back to her and sat with her. She might be alive if I'd done that."

"It was *Gott's* will she go home now."

Cherish looked down at Florence's suitcase. "Oh good. You're staying more than overnight?"

"I am. I'll stay until after the funeral and we'll go back together."

"Nee. I have to stay on. This place is mine now."

"Hmm. I don't know if you're old enough to own land in your own name. We'll have to find out."

"That's how Dagmar wanted it. Come on. Let's get out of the rain."

They moved onto the porch. "I know, but she might've thought you'd be a lot older when the time came."

"I don't know, Florence, I don't know."

Cherish looked like she was going to cry again, so

Florence said, "We'll talk about it all later. Show me where to put my suitcase."

"*Jah,* okay. I made up a bedroom for you." Cherish took Florence's suitcase and when Florence walked into the house, a strange sense of sadness came over her. The house smelled a little musty. She didn't remember if it had always been like that or whether the strange odor was coming from the wet clothes of the crowd of visitors. Even though she was tired, she forced a smile and walked forward to greet all the visitors who had gathered.

OVER BREAKFAST THE NEXT MORNING, Florence decided she had to get things sorted as quickly as possible, so they could both go home.

"Florence, I can run the farm. I know how to do everything. *Mamm* thinks of me as a child and I hope you don't."

"You are a child. I agree with *Mamm,* you're far too young." Florence sipped her coffee.

"I've got a good idea. You move here with me. It'd be such fun."

Florence shook her head. "*Nee.* That's a terrible idea. I'd be away from Carter and away from ..." Florence covered her mouth when she realized she cared for Carter even more than the orchard.

"So, you're in love with him?"

Florence didn't say anything. Remaining silent was answer enough. "I've got the orchard to look after."

Cherish sighed and then pushed her eggs around her plate with her fork. "I'm not leaving the farm. Someone will have to drag me away."

Florence ignored her response. "I'm calling Carter soon to see if he can collect us. Since this will be your place soon, you'll have to figure out who's going to look after it until you're old enough to do it yourself."

Cherish huffed. "I can't do that in one afternoon. Besides, we can't go before the funeral on Tuesday."

"How long would it take to find someone?"

"The Sunday meeting would be the best place to put the word out. It's Friday now, so that's only two more days. I could find someone at the meeting. Surely someone would know someone. I'll even call the bishop." She bounded to her feet. "I'll call him right now."

"What are you going to say?" Florence was pleased Cherish was putting all her energy into finding someone to take over the farm.

"I'm going to ask if he knows anyone who can be a caretaker here and look after the place until I'm old enough. They can live here for free and use everything as long as they look after all of Dagmar's things and all of her animals." She looked around. "I hate to leave it, but if you're going to force me, I'll have to."

"Okay, call him now."

Cherish wasted no time rushing out of the house. She hadn't even finished her breakfast.

Florence sat there, hoping again that her sisters wouldn't be too upset when they found out they'd been left out of Aunt Dagmar's will. It made sense, since Cherish had spent so much time with Dagmar. They probably wouldn't see things that way, though. It bothered Florence a little since she and her brothers were older and the first children of *Dat's* from his first wife. It was another thing that made Florence feel that she'd been bypassed – painted invisible – in favor of Wilma's girls.

CHAPTER 15

CHERISH WENT to the meeting on Sunday hoping and praying that today would be the day that they would find somebody to be the caretaker of her farm. It concerned her that the bishop couldn't think of anybody, because he knew so many people.

Before the meeting started, the bishop walked over to her. "How are you, Cherish?"

"I'm fine. Florence wants to leave to return home and I can't go with her if we don't have somebody to look after my Aunt's farm."

"That's exactly what I want to talk to you about."

"Really? Do you have a solution?"

"Better than that. I have someone I can recommend to live there permanently. At least for the foreseeable future."

"Perfect! Who is he, her, or them?" She giggled from sheer excitement.

"He's a man, and he's my nephew. He's visiting today from Little Creek. He wants to move this way to branch out on his own. Dagmar's place would be perfect for him. It's small enough for one person to farm on their own."

"That sounds perfect. When, um, how long will it take for him to get here?"

"He's already here. He arrived yesterday afternoon."

She looked over at the crowd of men and didn't see one stranger. "Where is he?"

The bishop turned around and looked about. "He must be outside. We've got time enough before the meeting starts. I'll take you so you can meet him."

She followed the bishop out of the house. "There he is." The bishop nodded to a tall gangly young man walking out of the barn. Immediately, she was disappointed. He only looked to be about the same age as she. How would he be responsible enough to watch over her farm?

"Malachi."

The young man looked up and hurried over. "Yeah?" He lifted up his chin.

"This is the young lady I've been telling you about. Cherish, meet Malachi."

He smiled and put his hand out and she shook it.

"Hello, Malachi."

"Hello, Charity."

"It's Cherish."

He frowned. "Never heard of that."

The bishop smiled. "I'll leave you two to talk."

"*Denke,*" said Cherish as the bishop turned and made his way into the house. She was so desperate to make this work that she looked past her initial negative reaction to Malachi. "Your *onkel* says you're interested in looking after my place. There's quite a lot to do, you know. The *haus* that has to be properly up-kept and there are many, many animals."

"I can do it."

"You might say that, but how do you know when you haven't seen it yet?"

He drew his dark eyebrows together. "Didn't Zachariah put in a good word for me?"

She studied his face. Did he think he was too old to still call his uncle, '*Onkel* Zachariah?'

"He did, that's true, but *I* don't know you." She folded her arms across her chest and decided to put him to the test. "Why don't you try and sell yourself to me?"

He stared down at her for a moment before he spoke. "I'll tell ya what. I'll stop by tomorrow and take a look at the place and then I'll tell ya if it suits me."

Cherish was horrified. He was her only hope. She put her hands by her sides when she decided the friendly approach was best. "Your *onkel* said you wanted a place to stay where you can be by yourself. Do you have any other options?"

He leaned forward. "Naw. Do you?"

She glared at the tall thin man. His ears stuck out

too far and he had a high forehead and she could only tell that because his hat was tilted back on his head – behind his ears. No one had bothered to iron his rumpled white shirt either. Looking down at his shoes, she saw they were spotless, obviously cleaned for the Sunday meeting. If only he'd taken that much care with the rest of him.

He followed her downward gaze. "What's wrong with me shoes?"

She looked into his piercing dark eyes, as black as a dark winter moonless night, and said, "Who said there was anything wrong with them?"

"Why were you staring at 'em?"

"I was just trying to work you out."

He narrowed his eyes as he studied her. "And you can do that by me shoes?"

"I can tell a lot about a person by their shoes and their clothes. You're obviously not married and I don't need your clean-shaven face to tell me that. I can see it by your crumbled clothes." She pinched the fabric of his sleeve between two fingers and then looked down at his crumpled black trousers. "Someone should've told you that you can still see wrinkles in dark fabric. If you had a woman in your life, she wouldn't allow you to leave the *haus* like you are." The friendly approach hadn't lasted long. When she had something in her head it always found a way out of her mouth.

"Did you say, *allow me?* I can tell you that when I get

married, I won't have no woman tellin' me what to do. I'll be the one doing the allowing."

"Good luck with that."

He sneered. "I don't need luck. Nothing is lucky or unlucky."

"I'd love to stay here and talk about your future unfortunate *fraa*, but I think the meeting's about to start." She turned and walked away. Within two strides, he was walking beside her.

"I've had a ton of experience in running farms by meself. Me other *onkel* has a dairy that needs three to run it and I handled it all by meself for four days running."

"I don't see how that's possible." She stopped and looked up into his face, admiring his high cheek bones, while he took off his hat and smoothed down his hair.

"Okay, it needed two to run, but nearly three people. I work hard and don't stop until the job's done. I can look after all animals you can name, even alpacas."

She grimaced. "We don't have those."

"If you did. I could look after 'em good."

"Look after them well," she corrected him, feeling superior. She'd ignored all his other incorrect words until she could take it no longer.

"Same difference." It didn't bother him. From his face, he seemed amused.

"It's not really."

"*Jah*, it is. It means the same thing. Anyway, you're

looking for someone good with animals not talkin,' aren't ya?"

For the first time in Cherish's life, she struggled to find words. The way he kept staring at her, she had to say something. "Let's talk again tomorrow at my place, shall we? At noon sharp." She walked ahead of him.

"Okay, but make it half past," he called after her.

She walked on, ignoring him.

She gave him one last look, took a deep breath in and blew it out, and then put her hands down by her side and walked into the bishop's house. She sat down next to Florence.

"Who was that I saw you talking with outside?"

"That was the bishop's nephew. The bishop thinks that he can look after the place for me, but I don't know."

"That's *wunderbaar.*"

Wasn't Florence listening? "He's coming tomorrow to look over the place, and I'll show him what to do and I'll see if I think he's up for the job."

"Well, it's not really a job. He's not going to get paid."

"Um, come to think of it, do you think he should be paid? There's a lot of work to do."

Florence whispered back, *"Nee!* We can't pay him.

He can keep the profits of the farm. I hope he can keep books."

"I don't think he'd be able to do much. Someone like him would be lucky to have a place to live at all. Anyway, that's the deal, he can take it or leave it." Cherish would've preferred someone older, even just a little older than Malachi, *but he can't be too terrible if the bishop suggested him.* When he walked into the house, she whispered to Florence, "There he is."

"Oh, he looks so handsome."

"I don't think so. Your taste is very different from mine."

"I don't see how anyone would think he isn't. He is very tall and manly looking – unusual, but in a good way. And just look at those dark eyes he's got."

Cherish continued to stare at him as he took his seat in the second row from the front. "He can't be very old."

"You're not very old and you're about to become the sole owner of a farm."

"That's right, I am. I still can't believe it. I don't know why Aunt Dagmar didn't tell me she was going to do that. *Gott* has blessed me."

"He certainly has."

Cherish leaned closer to Florence, and whispered, "He seems like the kind of person who would sit in one of the front rows. I've got him figured out already. I bet he's nice in front of his *onkel* because he's the bishop and not just because he's his *onkel* and…" Cherish stopped talking when one of the ministers stood to open the meeting in prayer.

When all eyes were closed, Cherish opened her eyes a crack to look at the bishop's nephew. She shut them tightly when she saw he'd turned around and was looking directly at her.

He was taking a risk that everyone else had their eyes closed for the prayer. She had to admire his courage and it satisfied her that he found her attractive. Why else would he be staring? Maybe they *could* work together. If he liked her, surely he'd do exactly what she said and would want to keep her happy. Every now and again she'd have to check up on him. Maybe Florence or *Mamm* could visit with her just to see that everything was going okay.

She opened her eyes and saw that he was still staring. Instead of closing her eyes this time, she frowned at him and he smiled. It was odd – well, *he* was odd. To make sure the smile was for her, she turned around and caught the girl behind her looking at him too.

Cherish faced the front at the same time that the minister finished his prayer. By that time, Malachi too was facing the front. The girl behind her was Annie Whiley. She was two years older and was the closest girl to her age in her aunt's community. Even so, they hadn't become friends. They had nothing in common.

CHAPTER 16

FLORENCE WALKED into the barn on Sunday night to make her regular phone call to Carter.

He answered with, "When are you coming home?"

She giggled. "I'll be home by the end of the week. The funeral's on Tuesday and Cherish has someone coming to see the place tomorrow – a potential care-taker. The bishop recommended him. He's also the bishop's nephew."

"Ah, nepotism."

"Not really. It's not a job or anything. He'll have to pay all the farm expenses and do all the work. What little there is left over, he'll get to keep."

"Make sure he's trustworthy."

"I'll be letting Cherish make the decision. She'll have to get used to doing that."

"Do you think that's wise?"

"I do. I think she's growing up fast. This responsibility she'll take on will make her mature quickly. I hope so anyway. She's going somewhere with the bishop tomorrow to sign papers."

"Somewhere?"

"To a lawyer's office."

"Ah."

"What have you been doing?"

"I've got a few business things happening. Otherwise, I'd come up to see you."

"Thanks, but it won't be necessary. I should only be a couple more days."

"I hope so. I've been missing you."

"Me too. I'm guessing you haven't heard from Wilma?"

"No. Should I have?"

"I was hoping she'd tell the girls about you. Maybe she's waiting until Cherish and I come home. That must be it." She heard Carter yawn. "Tired?"

"I'm minding Maggie's dog and he kept me awake. He takes up half the bed. No, more than half."

She giggled. "You have let the dog on your bed?"

"That's right."

"Didn't she have anyone else who could mind it?"

"No. She's from Nebraska. She's got no family around here. I offered when she mentioned she was looking for somewhere to leave him."

"Where's she gone?"

"Prison."

Florence didn't know what to say. This was one of

his workers. She seemed a bit posh too. "What? Why has she gone to prison?"

"Unpaid traffic fines. She said she paid them. There's some mixup. It'll all get sorted soon."

"I didn't know someone could go to jail for that."

"It's true."

"Well, it's nice of you to look after her dog."

"Spot and I are becoming good friends."

Florence heard Cherish calling her. "Cherish is yelling for me. I'll call you tomorrow."

"Okay. I miss you."

"Miss you too." She ended the call quickly, not liking the goodbye parts. She wanted to say she loved him, but wouldn't say it over the phone unless he said it first.

Florence walked back into the house and found Cherish was back in the kitchen, eating brownies.

"Where were you?"

"I was in the barn talking to Carter."

"Did you put money in the tin for the call?"

"*Nee.*" Florence laughed.

"It's not funny."

"Can't you spare your *schweschder* one phone call?"

"*Nee.* You've already had one call to Carter yesterday. I don't want to leave the new caretaker with a big phone bill."

"Fair enough." Florence sat down at the table with her. "I'll put enough money in tomorrow to cover all my calls." She stared at the brownies. "Where did you get them from?"

"From the meeting."

Florence then recognized the paper napkins as being the same ones from the meal after the meeting.

"Want some?"

"Okay. Just a bit. Just a bit of stolen brownie."

Cherish broke off a piece and handed it to her. "No one else was eating them. Oh, Florence, I don't know what to do. What if Malachi is no good? I have no one else."

"We'll have to hope that he is good. This brownie is really good – I can't believe no one was eating them. Are you excited about signing the papers tomorrow?"

"I'm nervous." Cherish looked around the kitchen. "What's weird is that we're sitting in Dagmar's home and she's not here. I feel she should be, and what should I do with all her things – her clothes, her books, her Bible?"

"Box up anything you want to keep and donate the rest. That's what we did when *Dat* died. *Mamm* kept his clothes for a while and then, a few weeks on, she was ready to let them go. She's still got a few boxes of his things in the attic. Sentimental things, I guess."

"We'll have to do that before we leave. I'll have to go through her things." Cherish sighed. "I'm not looking forward to it."

"Do you want me to help?"

"*Nee,* Florence. I'll do it alone. I'll wake up early and make a start on it before the bishop gets here."

"While you're doing that, I can feed the animals and do the milking, to give you more time."

"*Denke,* Florence."

CHAPTER 17

THE NEXT DAY, after Cherish had gone with Bishop Zachariah and signed the papers for the farm, Malachi arrived at a quarter after twelve.

The buggy he'd traveled in belonged to the bishop. Cherish walked out to meet him with hands on her hips. "Didn't I say be here at twelve?"

"I said I'd be here at twelve thirty, and I'm pretty sure I'm early." He tipped his hat and smiled at her. "You're welcome."

Reminding herself she had no one else, she shook off her irritation and dug out her manners. "Thanks for coming. I'll show you around."

"Yes please."

After she'd given him a quick tour, she stood outside the house. "Now I'll take you inside. What do you think? Can you do all this work every day? I don't want you to give up after a week and then I have to come back here."

"Cherish, I've got one thing to say."

She held her breath. Was he going to back out already? "And what's that?"

"It's not very organized. Lots of things are going on and there's too much work. If you reduced the number of animals …?"

"Everything must stay as it is. This is Aunt Dagmar's farm and for now it'll stay just as she had it."

FROM THE PORCH Florence had overheard their conversation and she cringed at the hardness in Cherish's voice. He did have a good point.

"Is that what you want?" he asked.

"It is. And, I am the owner. Or will be as soon as the paperwork goes through the official channels. I signed this morning."

He nodded. "Good to know. Well, do I have the job?"

"Give me a few moments to talk with Florence and if she thinks you're okay, I'll show you the *haus*. Wait right here."

Florence slipped back into the house, so Malachi wouldn't hear what they said. Cherish walked in and closed the door behind her. "What do you think, Florence?"

"I think he seems so nice, and a capable young man.

And even though he's the bishop's nephew, I don't think Bishop Zachariah would've recommended him if he didn't know he'd do a good job for you. Besides that, it'll be helping him out."

"I'm not a charitable organization, Florence. This is my farm we're talking about."

"I know that. I didn't say you were a charity. I'm just saying it could be a win-win, good for both of you."

Cherish rolled her eyes.

"And he did have a good point about reducing the variety of animals. It would be less work and probably be more profitable too."

"I'm not going to start right out by changing Dagmar's farm. It would be rude. Maybe changes can happen over time. I'll have to think about it."

Florence was pleased to see that her sister was open to different points of view. "If you don't give him the job as caretaker, there is no one else."

"We could both move here. You and me."

"I can't. I've got the orchard."

Cherish bit her lip. "That's right. And there's really no one else who can do what you do with it."

"Exactly. And Joy won't move away from Isaac, and I don't think it would be a good idea for you and Hope to live here. Two young girls on their own."

Cherish sighed and leaned her back against the wall. "There must be another answer."

"There's really not. *Gott* has handed this to you on a plate. Are you going to take it, or reject it?"

"Take it, I guess, but I'm really not happy about it. He seems bossy and opinionated. What if he tries to push me around?"

Florence laughed inside at the thought of someone trying to push Cherish around. They could try, but they wouldn't get very far. "I don't think he will. When you said you didn't want anything to change, he didn't protest. I think he'll take good care of the place."

"Do you?"

Florence nodded. "*Jah*, I do. Just tell him you're happy with him, and be friendly. You'll both have to get along."

"I wonder whether Dagmar would like a stranger being here."

"He's not a stranger, he's the bishop's nephew. And she's put the place in your hands to make the decision. She probably thought you'd be a lot older before you took the place over. I don't think she was expecting to die so suddenly."

"She might not have known what would happen, but *Gott* did," Cherish said.

Florence giggled. "Cherish, you're sounding more and more like Joy every day."

"I'm not meaning to, but sometimes you have to really look and see what's in front of you. Sometimes other people see what you can't. Okay, I'll take your opinions and advice. I'll tell him he can do it."

"I think that's best."

"You stay here. I'll tell him on my own."

That worried Florence. Cherish was only going to speak to him alone because she was going to say something that bordered on being unkind. "I think I should come along and hear what you have to say – and maybe an agreement should be written down."

"Okay. We'll work out what to say together, Malachi and I."

"Good. You tell him he can stay and I'll find pen and paper. We can work things out over a cup of something and a snack."

"*Denke*, Florence."

CHERISH WENT BACK OUTSIDE and walked over to Malachi, who was standing right where she'd left him. "I had a talk with Florence. She had her doubts, but I managed to talk her into it."

His stern face broke into a grin. "Glad to hear it." He reached out his hand and she shook it.

"Come into the *haus* and have a cup of coffee and a cookie." As they walked, she added, "Florence said we need to make a written agreement so we know exactly what to expect of each other."

"Okay. It sounds like a good idea." He laughed. "Sounds like we're getting married."

She rolled her eyes. "Don't be silly."

"I mean, the bit about what to expect of each other."

She ignored him until they were both seated at the kitchen table. "Florence?"

"I'm coming. Can you put the kettle on?"

"Okay." Cherish got up, filled the teakettle and started it heating, and then set out three mugs. Then she placed chocolate chip cookies onto a plate.

Florence walked in with pen and paper. "Okay, shall I write out what I think? And explain what I see as each of your obligations?"

"*Jah, denke,* Florence."

"Does anyone feel like a cup of coffee?" Cherish asked. "The water is hot."

"I'll have one," Florence said.

"Me too," added Malachi.

"How do you have your *kaffe,* Malachi?"

"Cream with two sugars."

"Of course you do." He couldn't be simple and have it black, could he? And he had to have cream and not just milk. Good thing Aunt Dagmar always kept a ready supply of both and they were nearly as good as fresh.

"I'm really in need of coffee. I missed my morning cup. Do you have a plunger or drip-filter coffee?"

"We have filter at home, but here it's the instant variety."

He pulled a face. "It's not real coffee."

She placed the jar down heavily on the countertop. "Do you want it or not?"

"Yeah, I'll have it."

When everyone had their coffee in front of them, Cherish set the cookies on the table and sat down. "It's so weird that Aunt Dagmar's gone and this is my place now."

Timmy, the blue budgerigar, chirped as though he agreed with her. She walked over to Timmy's cage at the back of the room. She pulled him out and placed him on her shoulder, the same as Dagmar had done at least a couple of times a day.

"I think I'll take you home with me, Timmy."

"That'd be good. One less mouth to feed," Malachi said with a laugh before he slurped his coffee. "I've never seen a bird do that." He stared at the bird on her shoulder.

"Now you've seen it." She could feel Florence staring at her and that reminded her to be friendly toward him. "I'm sorry if I'm sounding rude, Malachi. I'm not normally like this. I've had no sleep for days and I'm so upset about Dagmar. I don't know how I'm going to get through the funeral tomorrow."

"I understand. It must be a stressful time for you. Let me know if I can do anything to help."

"Just look after this place as though it were your own." When she noticed his shirt was wrinkled, despite their conversation yesterday, she said, "Or perhaps, look after it as though it were someone else's."

"I'll do a fine job, Charity. Don't you worry about that."

How hard is it to remember my name? She remembered his. "It's Cherish."

He laughed. "Sorry, Cherish."

She sipped on her hot coffee to stop herself saying something she'd later regret.

CHAPTER 18

WHILE THEY SAT DRINKING coffee and eating cookies, Florence ended up having to re-write the agreement three times, until both parties agreed on the contents. When they had both signed it, Florence said, "After the funeral, I'll find somewhere in town to copy it and then you can each keep a copy and I'll keep one too. I'm sure it's nothing legal, but it will keep both of you on track if disagreements about anything arise."

"Fair enough," Malachi said.

"*Denke*, Florence."

He looked over at Cherish. "When do you want me to move in?"

"When can you?"

"Whenever you want."

"Wednesday?"

"Sure thing."

"No wait. I'll need a whole day to explain to you

what to do. Why don't you spend the whole day Wednesday and we'll go through everything from morning to night, and then you move in the day after. That'll be Thursday. Before you move in, you have to know exactly how to do everything. Do you have a good memory?"

"The best. Can I have another cup of coffee?"

"You liked it?"

"It wasn't bad."

She got up and relit the stove. It wouldn't take long for the warm water to boil again.

"I'll walk you around now and show you again where everything is and tell you what needs to be done. I'll also leave you money for expenses until you start getting money coming in. You should take notes on everything I say."

"I will. I'll come here after the funeral too, to learn more. Good thing that *Onkel* Zachariah is having the viewing and the after-funeral meal at his *haus*." He chuckled.

It annoyed Cherish when he laughed. Was he mocking her? She rose to her feet. "Come along. I'll show you some more of what to do now. That'll give it time to soak into your brain. You won't have so much to remember all at once."

Florence stood. "I'm sure you two have got things to talk about. I'll take a walk."

"Now?"

"*Jah*. I won't go far. Don't worry."

Cherish watched Florence walk away, not happy about being left alone with the stranger.

"Can't you hear it?"

"What?" she snapped.

"The kettle. It's whistling."

"Oh. Yes." She walked away and made his instant coffee with two sugars and cream. Then she stirred it so the sugar would dissolve.

"White sugar?"

She jumped. She hadn't noticed him walking toward her. "What other kind is there?"

"Loads of other kinds. I was just thinking, if it's instant coffee, honey might taste better."

"Yuck. That would be dreadful. I think so, anyway."

"Don't worry. Is it done?"

She handed the mug to him, deliberately holding onto the handle so he'd have to touch the hot part of it.

He took it from her. *"Denke."* Then he eyed her suspiciously as he quickly switched his grasp to the handle and blew on the other hand to ease the burning sensation.

"Let's go." She walked out of the house, realizing he'd noticed her rude behavior.

She showed him where the food was stored for the different animals, and talked through all the feeding routines.

"It's pretty much standard," he said when she'd finished.

"You said you were going to write it down."

"Little difficult with my coffee." He set the empty mug down on the ground.

"I'll write it all down anyway so if you forget it, it'll be there for you."

"Okay. Thank you."

"I wish I could live here." She put her hands on her hips and looked around, wishing she was just a year or two older, or maybe three. If she was eighteen then 'they' might allow her to live there. It would be lonely, but she would've talked one of her sisters into coming with her.

"Why can't you?"

She shook her head. "I'm obviously not old enough."

"How old are you?"

Why was age so important to everyone and why did everyone ask her age? She hadn't been rude enough to ask him his age, but she would now. "Well, how old are you?"

"Twenty-two, but I'm mature minded, I've been told."

He answered that too quickly. She stared at his smooth skin. "You look a lot younger."

"Well you look a lot older."

She smirked at him. "I haven't even told you how old I am."

"I'm guessing you're twelve."

"Twelve!" she shrieked. "How rude."

He put his head to the side and smiled. "Truthfully, I reckon you're about fifteen or sixteen."

"Well it's none of your business anyway." She looked down at the mug he'd placed on the ground. Was he going to pick that up or just leave it there? Was he someone who lived like an untidy, slovenly pig?

"I believe anyone under eighteen can't enter into a contract."

"We don't have a contract between us. It is simply an agreement between ourselves, nothing legal. Oh, were you talking about the contract for the land and the house? Because I found out I can—"

"I'm talking about our contract between us. As long as you're not going to change things on me, it'll be fine."

"Of course I won't. And if you're not happy at any time, you can always give me at least a few days' notice, like it says in our agreement, and then leave."

"I'll stay." He looked around. "This place suits me fine ... for now. And, when are you leaving?"

"We'll leave on the day you move in."

"Suits me. I'll be sorry to see you go." He offered a lopsided grin.

She frowned at him. "I'll give you our phone number before I go."

"And where does that go to? A shanty outside your house? Will you be the one answering when I call, or some neighbor ... and then you'll have to call me back, and then I won't be around." He looked down and moved his feet around in the dirt.

"No. Our phone's in our own barn. We're a big enough family that one or the other of us generally hears it ringing."

"Fair enough. I'll give you weekly phone updates. If you answer the phone when I call – if not, I won't bother."

"Thank you, that would be good. Try a second time, though, if you don't get an answer right away. We own a large apple orchard, so it can take some time to get to the phone if we're busy. And, I'll visit every so often." She looked down at the coffee cup. She'd never get away with doing that at home. "Just to see how nicely you're keeping the place."

He nodded.

"You can start your duties by putting this back inside." She bent down, picked up the mug and handed it to him.

"Sorry about that." He took it from her and then looked at her.

"Well, go on. Into the kitchen." She made shooing motions with her hands and he walked away. When movement caught her eye, she turned and saw Florence walking back up the driveway. When Florence had nearly reached her, they both stood still when they noticed a car turning up the driveway. Cherish hurried to Florence, hoping it was *Mamm* coming to stay for the funeral.

"It's Mark," Florence said.

Cherish was overjoyed and ran to the car causing it to stop before it reached the house.

"Mark, I can't believe you came."

He got out of the car and hugged his sisters. Then he pulled his suitcase out of the back seat. "Of course I would. It's an emergency and I had to make sure both you girls are okay."

"We are fine," said Florence.

"Remember, Florence? I was just saying the other day that I miss *Dat* and Mark." Cherish turned to their brother. "You remind me so much of *Dat.*"

He chuckled. "Maybe because I'm his son?"

"You know what I mean. It's nice having a man around the house." Malachi walked out and Mark stared at him. Cherish followed his gaze to see Malachi.

"This is Malachi. He's the caretaker. Oh, I didn't tell you – have you told him, Florence?"

"I haven't said anything to anyone."

Cherish looked at Mark. "Aunt Dagmar left me her house – the whole farm – and before going home we needed to hire a caretaker. This man is the caretaker."

"Well, I wasn't expecting that news."

Malachi drew level with them, and Florence introduced the two men.

"I'm pleased to meet you, Malachi."

"Me too. I'll do a good job here for all of you."

"It's not their place, it's mine. So, you'll be doing a good job for me," Cherish told him.

Mark gave a low chuckle. "How does it feel to be the owner of the farm, Cherish?"

"It feels like I'm in a dream. But, the dream would've been better if Aunt Dagmar was still here."

Malachi grunted. "It wouldn't be yours if she was here."

"Obviously. But I'd rather her be here."

Florence put her hand on her shoulder. "I know what you mean, but you'll see her again someday."

"Not too soon I hope." Malachi laughed at his own words.

Cherish looked at him and pulled a sour face.

He cleared his throat and looked at Mark. "Have you been here before?"

"I've been here, but it was many years ago."

Cherish grabbed Mark's arm. "I'll show you around."

"While she's doing that, I'll take your suitcase into the *haus*."

"*Denke,*" Mark said.

When Mark and Cherish left, Florence felt like she had to apologize for the way her sister acted, but at the same time, she didn't want to undermine Cherish in anyway.

He took off his hat and ruffled his hair. "She's a feisty one."

"She is. She means well."

"Does she?"

"Yes, she does. She's got a good heart."

"You'd know, being her sister and all. She doesn't want me to make any changes around here. I told her that I thought it would be better to have … Well, to concentrate on a couple of things." He shook his head. "I've got bees for the honey, eggs to sell, a little milk to sell, from both cows and goats … all of that makes for a lot of work. A lot of varied work, now if—"

"It's no use talking to me about it. You're probably right, but I'm sure Cherish just wants things how Dagmar left them, at least for a while."

"I know, she said that, but I thought you might be able to talk some sense into her."

"I've never been successful at that so far. I run an orchard, so I don't know much about this sort of farming. Cherish knows more because she's stayed with Dagmar a lot over the past two years."

He chuckled. "Like that, is it?"

"I'm afraid so."

He looked over at Cherish. "How old is she?"

"Not old enough for you to be thinking about her in any other way than the owner of this place."

He looked surprised by Florence's comment. "Believe me, I wasn't thinking of anything like that. I would pick someone more … someone quieter. Someone with less opinions about things." He shrugged his shoulders. "Anyway, that's not why I came to this community."

"Why did you come?"

He looked down at the ground as though he didn't

want to say. Florence guessed that he was escaping from something. It couldn't have been too bad, otherwise the bishop wouldn't have recommended him.

"That's okay, you don't have to say. We all have our own reasons for doing things and they don't have to make sense to other people."

He offered an embarrassed, grateful smile and then picked up the suitcase. As they walked to the house, Florence asked, "Do you have siblings?"

"I do. Too many to count. They won't even notice I'm gone." He laughed.

When Mark got back to the house with Cherish, Malachi left.

"CHERISH, can you make up another bedroom for Mark?"

"Of course. It's weird having my own place now." She hurried off leaving Mark in the kitchen alone with Florence.

"Now I can tell you the real reason I came."

Real reason? Florence stared at him wondering if it was a joke. "Other than what you told us, you mean?"

He nodded. "The reason I'm here is twofold. First, I am here for the funeral, of course, and the second reason is because Wilma's worried."

"About Cherish? I haven't even told her about Dagmar leaving the farm to her."

"Not that. She said you're leaving to marry an *Englischer*. I said she must've heard you wrong."

She gulped. She had never thought she'd be in this position, but here she was. About to walk out on her family, and they might reject her forever. "It's true. He lives next door and we've talked for a couple of years now since he moved in. We met when his cows broke into our orchard. I've spent time with him and we've fallen in love."

He shook his head and couldn't look at her. "I never believed it."

"I'm in love. I've never felt like it before."

"Wait for the man *Gott* has for you. There's still time."

She had hoped that Mark would understand. "I believe Carter is the man He has for me."

"The devil has deceived you." This time he looked her right in the eyes and she didn't know how to respond.

"I know you don't understand, Mark. If I was hearing my story from someone else I wouldn't understand either. It's not as though I woke up one morning and just decided I'd like to go through a great deal of hardship and upset my family by marrying an *Englisher*."

"But that's what you're doing, *jah?*"

"That's what I'm doing."

He shook his head. "Don't do it."

"I am."

"When were you going to tell me?"

"I'm not sure. I've got so many things to think about, and then this emergency came up with Aunt Dagmar being ill."

"The family needs you."

"I've given so much of myself. Now it's my time."

"That's selfish."

She shrugged her shoulders. "When do I get to be happy – have a family of my own? Since *Dat* died, and you and Earl left home, Wilma has put practically everything on my shoulders. The years are passing me by, Mark. I'll never get them back. I don't want to look back on my life and regret not snatching my one chance at love and holding onto it for dear life." She hoped he'd understand.

"You're making a mistake."

Cherish bounced into the room and said with a sing-song voice. "Room's ready." She looked at the two of them and the smile left her face. "What's going on?"

"Mark's heard about my decision to leave."

Cherish sat down. "She hasn't left yet. There's still hope that she won't. Even if she does leave, she can always come back."

"I want an easier path for her."

"I know you do, Mark, but I must make my own decisions."

"Or mistakes," Cherish added with a bright smile.

CHAPTER 19

THE NEXT FEW days went quickly, with Aunt Dagmar's funeral, and then Cherish showing Malachi what to do with the farm.

It was Friday morning when the driver arrived to take the three of them home.

The journey seemed much longer to Florence than the journey to Dagmar's even though it was the same distance.

When they were nearly home, Florence looked over to see Mark had fallen asleep.

"*Denke* for coming to help me, Florence. I mean coming out here to be with me while I sorted all of Aunt Dagmar's things out."

"Of course. I was happy to do that. You'd do the same for me. I didn't do much. The bishop did most of it. Taking you to the bank and sorting all the paperwork out with the lawyer."

Cherish took a deep breath. "I don't think I could've coped without you there."

"We all help each other."

Cherish went back to looking out the window and Florence regretted putting her needlework in her bag in the trunk. The drive was so long, she needed something to do. Although, last time she sewed in the car it did give her motion sickness.

Cherish suddenly said, "Do you remember *Mamm* said something about having a surprise to tell us?"

"I do. I remember it very well."

"She never told us anything. I wonder what it was about."

"Why don't you ask her when we get home?" Finally, *Mamm* was going to tell them about Carter, and it was good that Cherish was going to be the one to remind her.

"I love surprises." Cherish adjusted the blanket over Timmy's cage that was by her feet. "I hope she doesn't mind me bringing Timmy. She doesn't like animals very much."

"I'm sure she won't mind. And as Malachi said, it's one less animal for him to look after."

"Not that a little bird like this takes much caring for."

"It's a good thing we didn't bring Caramel. It would've been a bit squishy on the way back."

Cherish giggled. "That's true."

"I'm sure the bird will like having so much fuss

made of him. I don't know if Malachi would've had much time to speak to him."

"*Nee*, I don't think he would've bothered. I got the idea Malachi didn't like Timmy very much. Neither did I, until I got to know him."

Florence put her head back and closed her eyes. When she opened them next, they were at Mark's house. Their good-byes were subdued.

When the car pulled up at their house, Florence was glad to be home, but … for how much longer would it be her home?

ALL THREE GIRLS and *Mamm* came running to the car. Cherish got out of the car and held up the birdcage. "I had to bring Timmy home, *Mamm*. Is that okay?"

"It's the least we could do, to look after Dagmar's pet bird."

Cherish covered the bird over again. "You don't mind?"

"I don't mind at all." *Mamm* hugged Cherish and then each of the girls fussed over her.

"We didn't bring Dagmar's dogs. We thought it would be too many dogs."

"Besides, they're used to it there on the farm," Florence said.

"Where's Caramel?"

"Upstairs asleep I think," *Mamm* said.

"They both sleep in my bed when they're having a

nap during the day," said Joy, "and at night I make them sleep on the floor in the blanket. They curl up together. Isn't that sweet?"

"*Denke,* for looking after Caramel, Joy."

Joy smiled. "Everyone helped."

They still hadn't told the family that Aunt Dagmar had left Cherish the farm, and Florence hoped Wilma would be okay about that.

WHEN JOY HAD MADE hot tea, they all sat down in the living room.

"One thing we haven't said anything about is Aunt Dagmar's will," Florence said.

"When does that all get sorted out?" *Mamm* asked.

"We sorted that out before we left."

Mamm's face contorted. "What do you mean?"

"The reason we took so long coming back was that Aunt Dagmar left everything she owned to Cherish."

Everyone looked at Cherish, totally surprised.

"It's true. I am the property owner."

"And you signed papers?" Joy asked.

"I have. Bishop Zachariah took me to the lawyer's office, and he's cosigner because I'm young and that's what Aunt Dagmar wanted."

Mamm's eyebrows drew together as she stared at Florence. "Why didn't you tell me this?"

"I wasn't deliberately keeping it from you. It was just that there was so much going on with trying to keep everything going on the farm, and getting a good caretaker in to look after the place."

"And, did you?"

"*Jah*, we got someone. He's the bishop's nephew. Bishop Zachariah recommended him and he seems nice – capable and everything. He's done that kind of work before."

"So, he'll live there and look after the farm?" asked Joy.

"He will. And when I'm old enough to move there I will."

"You'd move there, away from us?" Hope asked.

"Only when I'm older, and not before then."

Mamm shook her head and muttered something under her breath.

"Are you alright, *Mamm?*" asked Favor.

"I am, but it seems unfair to me. There are six girls and she leaves everything to one."

"Seven girls," Florence corrected her.

"Oh, yes. That's right. Seven girls."

Florence said, "She was my – our – *vadder's schweschder.* You have six *dochders*, but Aunt Dagmar had seven nieces. And two nephews, don't forget."

"I know that, Florence. It's not always about you."

"It's never about me, or Mark, or Earl. Maybe Earl would've liked to live on Dagmar's farm. He certainly doesn't feel he fits in around here."

Cherish gasped. "I'm sorry. I didn't even think to ask Earl."

"Don't worry about it," said Florence. "He seems quite settled, where he is. I was just using that as an example."

Mamm eyed Cherish. "And did you know she was leaving the farm to you, Cherish? Did she tell you she was going to do that? Or, did you encourage her? You can be persuasive."

"I had no idea at all. I was shocked when I found out. The bishop was the one who told me. Otherwise, I never would've known."

"You can always sell it," said Hope. "When you're older, you can sell it and buy something here."

"Maybe. I'll have to wait and see. Right now, I like it out there. It's so quiet and peaceful with just me and the animals and wildlife."

"I think Dagmar should've told me she was thinking of doing that. I should've been consulted."

"It's possible, and I've said this to Cherish, that she might've thought she had many more years and by that time, Cherish would've been an adult."

Favor said, "It made sense to leave it to Cherish. We don't even know her very well."

"I knew her well," *Mamm* snapped.

"Let's talk about something else, shall we?" Joy suggested.

"Jah!" Mamm nodded emphatically.

Florence caught Cherish's eye and gave her a look to remind her about the surprise *Mamm* had said she was going to share.

It didn't take Cherish long to catch on. *"Mamm,* before I left here you were talking about a secret you were going to share with us all."

Wilma looked around at all of them and lastly at Florence. "Not all of you might be happy about this, but I do have some news to share with you all. It's something unexpected, but I hope you'll all be happy about it."

Florence looked at all their faces. The girls had no idea what Wilma was going to say. Her sisters would feel much better about her marrying Carter when they learned he was Wilma's nephew and their cousin. Florence was still ever so thankful that Carter was no relative of hers.

"What is it, *Mamm?"*

"Jah tell us."

Mamm giggled, like a girl. "Okay, but don't be shocked."

"We'll try not to be," Joy said.

"Okay, well…" *Mamm* hesitated, then blurted out, "I'm getting married."

CHAPTER 20

THERE WAS stunned silence and Florence was devastated. Wilma was supposed to tell the girls about Carter. This supposed good news was terrible – the worst news ever.

The first to speak was Joy. "Who are you marrying?"

Florence didn't need to ask, she knew who it was. The same man who'd been showing interest in her for years.

"It's Levi Bruner," Florence said when *Mamm* hesitated again.

Hope clapped her hands. "That's *wunderbaar*. That means Bliss will be our half-*schweschder.*"

"Step-*schweschder,*" said Florence. "You don't share either parent, so it's not half-sister."

"It seems I must've missed a lot when I've been away," Cherish said, not looking impressed. "What happens to us?"

"When is the wedding happening?" Favor asked.

"Are you sure about this, *Mamm?*" Joy asked.

Mamm giggled. "You're all talking at once."

Florence cleared her throat, wondering about her own second love – the orchard. "That's good news, *Mamm*, and when will you be married?"

"We haven't set a time yet. But I don't see any reason to wait much longer. Everything's happening so quickly around here."

"Will we have to move *haus?*" asked Favor. "Because I'll have to tell my penpals my new address. I don't know that Levi's *haus* is big enough for us all."

"*Jah,*" Hope said. "I'm already using two bedrooms now. I'm not going back to sharing one. Well, I will if I have to, but I'd rather not."

"Your lives won't change. We won't be moving. Bliss and Levi are moving here. We'll have to find Bliss a nice bedroom. Hope, you might have to go back to using one bedroom."

Hope pouted.

"I can still run the orchard, and the store in the harvest season. Will that be okay?" Florence still didn't know if her family was going to turn their backs on her.

"We've talked about this a great deal and Levi would like to try his hand at running the orchard. With you leaving the community, Florence, it couldn't have worked out better in the timing."

Was that a joke? Florence stared at *Mamm* and there

was no hint of a smile on Wilma's face. "You can't be serious?"

"*Jah,* I am."

"Running an orchard is not something you *try* your hand at. Especially an orchard that's as intricate as ours. We have worked so hard to get the organic accreditation and there are strict rules to follow to enable us to keep it. I know what I'm doing, and only because I've studied it for years alongside *Dat.*"

"*Mamm,* you can't make Levi boss over Florence. Sure, let him work in the orchard, but Florence is right. She's the only one who really knows what she's doing around here."

"I have no intention of making Levi boss over her. Florence said she's leaving. Didn't you hear that?"

"I am marrying Carter, but that doesn't mean I'm leaving the orchard. I had hoped we could work something out, after all, the orchard's mine." She probably should've stopped there, but the rest spilled out of her mouth. "So is this *haus,* and so is the land."

"That's where you're wrong," *Mamm* said. "This house, the orchard and the land is not yours, it's mine."

Florence's mouth fell open and she desperately hoped that wasn't true. She was convinced that the orchard was hers since her two brothers were not interested in it. And she and her two brothers were the only *kinner* from *Dat's* first marriage. "The orchard belonged to my *mudder* and *vadder.* It should come down to me,

Mark and Earl. They don't want it, and they're happy for me to have it."

"I'm sorry to tell you Florence, it's mine. Everything goes to the *fraa* when her husband dies."

That was dreadful news to Florence. Unreasonable. Shocking! "The orchard's not mine?"

"*Nee*, Florence, it's mine. I did view it as ours, but you're leaving and you'll leave with nothing." She paused to drive that home, "You can stay and show Levi what to do if you want to, but then you should go."

"Can't I work the orchard, same as always? I won't want payment."

Mamm shook her head. "It wouldn't be a good example to the girls."

"But we want Florence to stay," Cherish said. "Nothing'll get done without her. She's the wheels that keep the cogs of this place moving."

Hope, sitting next to her, pulled on her arm. "Won't you stay, Florence?"

Mamm spoke before Florence had a chance. "Once I marry Levi, Florence can no longer live here."

Florence couldn't believe it – she was being kicked out of her own home.

"And I strongly believe that you should go to the bishop and make your leaving official, Florence. You can't stay around the community with one foot in and one foot out. You've told the girls you're leaving to marry this outsider, so you should either do it or not do it, and not just talk about it."

Florence looked at her stepmother in disbelief at her cold-heartedness. "So, either way you don't want me around?"

"You're acting lukewarm and you know what the Bible says about a person who's lukewarm. Tell her, Joy."

"*Nee, Mamm.* I will always want Florence to stay here, forever. As long as she wants."

"Then, you'd be putting your own salvation in harm's way." She looked back at Florence. "I have to take a stand, Florence, for the sake of my girls."

Florence stood up. She knew the tears would soon flow. *Her girls?* She always knew that Wilma didn't see her as one of 'her girls.' "I can't believe my ears. I wonder what *Dat* would say about all this right now?"

Mamm snapped back, "He'd be upset, and ashamed of you for leaving the community."

Florence sat back down, willing back the tears. She wouldn't let them flow in front of anyone. "Since you're being so honest, why don't you tell the girls a bit more about Carter? Tell them who his mother is."

Mamm shook her head. "*Nee*, Florence. Don't speak about it."

"Go on, tell them since you're being so full of self-righteousness."

Wilma's shoulders lowered. "It's not what you think."

"The girls should know. Shall I be the one to tell them about Carter and who he really is?"

"*Nee,* Florence."

"They deserve to know the truth and Carter deserves the truth out in the open. If you don't tell them right now, Wilma, I will."

"The man next-door is not Iris's child. I've been meaning to talk to you about it. Let's not say more in front of everyone. I'll talk to you in private."

"*Nee,* we want to hear," Favor said.

Florence felt she was going to pass out; she couldn't take any more surprises. Carter told her he was Iris's child and if he was lying to her, it didn't make sense. How would he have even known about Iris? "I don't understand."

"I can't say it any plainer. The man next-door is not Iris's child."

"How could you know that for sure?"

In the background, the girls were asking, "Who's Iris?" among themselves.

Florence knew Carter wouldn't lie to her. "He's not making it up. How would he know about Iris and why would he lie about it?"

"I've no doubt he thinks he knows what he's told you is the truth."

"*Mamm,* who's Iris?" Joy asked.

Florence still thought it best Wilma tell them, so she remained silent.

"I didn't want to tell you this way, but Florence is forcing me."

The girls stared at Florence. "I'm not forcing you to do anything, *Mamm.* They should probably know. They *deserve* to know the truth."

"Iris was my *schweschder.* She left the community and … I just found out days ago that she'd died a few years ago. I hadn't seen her for years. Since she came here when Mercy was a *boppli.* I thought she was alive somewhere. I didn't even imagine for one moment that she was dead."

"We never knew you had a *schweschder,*" Joy said.

"I never said anything about her. She was disowned by all when she left."

Florence sighed, growing impatient. "What about Carter?"

"I'm getting to that."

While *Mamm* sat there wringing her hands in her lap, Florence's mind went to the worst possible places.

Was Carter Wilma's illegitimate son? Or worse, was he Wilma and her father's child, born out of wedlock? She knew now that Carter was older than she was by two years. *Mamm* had lied about so many things. "Just tell us the truth please."

"I was never going to say anything else."

"Carter believes Iris is his mother," Florence said once more.

"That's because she raised him."

Florence did her best to steady her nerves. "Whose son is he, really?"

Wilma looked around at the girls. "I didn't want to say this, but at least I'm glad now that it's out in the open. Before your father and I ...."

"Just tell me, *Mamm*. Is Carter my half-*bruder*?"

CHAPTER 21

As usual, the words had stumbled out of Florence's mouth before she could stop them, but she had to know. It would ruin her life if Carter was a half-sibling. The girls were now all wide-eyed, staring at Wilma and waiting for her next words.

Wilma shook her head. *"Nee,* Florence. He's not *your* half-sibling, but he's a half-siblings to you girls." She stared at her daughters. "Your *vadder* knew about him. I told him before we married that I had a son somewhere. It didn't change his feelings about me. I named him Joseph. Iris must've changed his name."

"I don't understand," Favor said. "There's only the six of us. What son?"

"Who did you name 'Joseph?' You had a son?" Cherish asked.

"I think *Mamm's* saying she had a *boppli* with someone, a man who wasn't *Dat,* before she got married."

"That's right, Joy. I made a mistake and that mistake was Carter."

Florence narrowed her eyes. No child should ever be called a mistake.

"I had a child before I married your *vadder*. I told him of my sin, but I didn't want anyone in the community to know. I was able to hide my enlarged body under big dresses. When the birth drew near, I told my family Iris had called and wanted to come back and I was fetching her. They didn't want me to go and forbade me. I had to go. I left in the middle of the night on foot and got a ride into town. I called Iris and told her the mess I was in and she took me to the doctor. He said I was days away from giving birth. I had guessed I was close. I sent a message to my family that I'd be home soon and that I was hoping to bring Iris back with me. It was all lies, but what was I to do? I ended up going back alone and telling them Iris changed her mind about coming home."

Joy shook her head.

"I know you're disappointed in me, Joy."

"*Nee, Mamm.* I'm shocked that you've never told us."

"Then what happened?" Favor asked, as she left her chair to sit at *Mamm's* feet.

"When he was born, Iris begged me to keep him. I wouldn't. How could I? She said she'd take him, and that suited me fine. It was either adopt him out or give him to someone I knew. He would be safe with Iris. She was a good person, with a loving heart."

"*Mamm*, you told me she came to the door once and that was the last time you saw her. When was that?"

"It was when Mercy was a *boppli*. She was in town and she begged me to see the child. I refused and told her never to come back." She shook her head. "I never saw her again."

"Carter spent his whole life thinking that Iris was his *mudder* when all along it was you?" Hope asked.

Wilma nodded. "I think so." Her eyes glistened with tears. "I'm glad the truth's out. It's been a burden to bear all these years. I hope you girls don't feel different about me now."

Florence sat there, stunned, taking it all in. It had to be the truth. Wilma wouldn't have told lies putting herself in a bad light.

Joy shook her head. "I'm just shocked. It's odd for us to be hearing about this now. We have a *bruder* that we've never met. I mean we know who he is, but we didn't know who he was."

"And he's been living next door to us," Hope added.

Mamm nodded. "All I can say is that I'm sorry. That's why I was so harsh with you, Cherish. I sent you away to the farm because I didn't want you to end up like … to make a mistake like I did. I liked the male attention when I was young just like you do. I made a mistake I could not take back."

Florence thought back to the letters from Gerald Braithwaite. "Wait a minute. You had an affair with Gerald Braithwaite, your *schweschder's* husband?"

The girls fell silent.

"*Nee*. It's not like that, Florence. *Jah*, he's Carter's *vadder*, but he didn't know who Iris was then. I was the one who gave him Iris's phone number, later, so he could see his child."

"He didn't want him either?" Hope asked.

"The poor little unwanted *bu*." Favor shook her head.

"He was wanted by Iris," *Mamm* said. "I offered him the child, but he said he couldn't raise him alone. He wanted to keep in contact with our son, but after I gave him Iris's number, I told him to never contact me again. I told Iris to take the *boppli* and go. I never wanted to see any of them again. I wanted them out of my heart and out of my mind."

"Were you in love with that man, *Mamm?*" Hope asked.

"At the time, I thought so." She looked at Florence. "When I was at Carter's place with you the other day, I realized that Gerald had married Iris. I never knew that until then."

"So, the letters were to you, *Mamm?* The letters from Gerald that I found in the attic, they were your letters? Not to my mother, and not to Iris?"

"That's right. Back then, I had to fib to Gerald and tell him I was about to marry someone from the community, or he wouldn't have let me alone. Then, when I had the child, I contacted him."

"And then you had to fib again to tell Florence they

weren't your letters?" Joy asked. "More lies. That's the trouble with one lie, you have to tell more and more of them to make people believe the first one."

"You're right, Joy. I learned that the hard way."

"Tell us everything from the start, *Mamm*. Where did you meet the man who's the *vadder* of our half-*bruder?*"

"I'd rather not go into it. It was a lifetime ago. I'm not the same person as the person who did that."

"We're not judging you, *Mamm*, but since you've kept this from us for so long, won't you tell us the story?" Hope asked from her seated position on the floor.

"I think it will upset her," Florence said.

"Nothing can upset me now. Make us some more tea, Joy, and I'll tell the whole story."

"From the beginning, please," Favor said.

Florence shook her head. "Carter doesn't know the truth. He's convinced Iris was his mother. *Mamm*, you'll have to tell him the truth."

Mamm shook her head. "I couldn't face him again, the child I gave away. You'll have to tell him."

JOY JUMPED up and went to the kitchen; she'd heard enough. After she popped the kettle onto the flame, she lined up clean cups and saucers onto a tray. Then she stared outside wondering when Isaac would arrive. Not before *Mamm* finished telling them what happened, she

189

hoped. Joy couldn't deny she felt slightly – no, more than slightly – betrayed and deceived by not knowing the truth sooner. It was amazing that *Mamm* had held the truth in for so long. If Florence hadn't gotten involved with the man next door, they might never have learned the truth. And, not only that, Carter didn't even know the truth.

Cherish walked in to help her, bringing their used cups to the sink. They divided the clean cups onto two trays, along with the fixings, while waiting for the water to boil. When the tea was brewed, they both carried trays of tea items to the living room.

Once they all had tea and were settled again, Favor said, "Tell us, *Mamm*."

She gave a huge sigh. "I was seventeen. I met him at the farmers market. Really, he was more of a man than a boy. I lied about my age and we had a few dates in secret. I was rebellious like Cherish."

"I wondered who I took after." Cherish grinned.

"This isn't funny, Cherish." Joy glared at her.

"I know. Shush, let *Mamm* tell the story."

"He knew I had to see him in secret because I was Amish. One day, one thing led to another and ... I ended up in a situation." *Mamm's* bottom lip trembled.

"Go on," Joy urged.

"He wanted to marry me when I told him about the baby. Before that he'd sent letters and when I didn't answer them, he came out to the farm to try and see me.

I wasn't home at the time and my *vadder* wasn't happy and wanted to know why a man wanted to see me. I told *Dat* the man was mixed up and was really looking for Iris. He seemed to believe that. That's when I wrote to Gerald to tell him I was marrying an Amish man. Then the letters came back begging me not to marry. Those are the letters you saw, Florence." She looked at the girls. "Just because I made a mistake I don't want you girls to think you can do whatever you like. There are consequences."

"Then you'll have to cut all these lies out, *Mamm*. Face your past and tell Carter the truth." Joy folded her arms.

"I can't. I can't face him."

"You should force yourself. People have to know the truth. Don't they deserve that much?"

Tears streamed down *Mamm's* face. "I can't do it."

"I'll come with you," Joy said.

"When do we get to meet him?" Hope asked. "I've never met him."

"I have," said Cherish.

Joy jumped up and stormed out of the room, so Florence sat next to *Mamm* and put her arm around her. "It's okay. I'll tell him."

"*Denke*, Florence. Tell him I'm sorry. I didn't know that he wouldn't have been told. I didn't know that Gerald was going to marry Iris. I didn't know that Iris was going to tell him she was his mother. I just hoped she wouldn't tell him that I was. I wanted to put that baby out of my mind forever. I always wondered about him, though."

JOY CAME BACK into the living room and said, "I'll have to tell Isaac. We don't have secrets."

"*Nee*, you can't. It's my secret and I don't want to bring shame upon the *familye*."

"I can't keep it from him."

"You'll have to."

Joy huffed. This was putting her in a dreadful situation. She didn't make her mother's mistake, but now she felt a part of it. She was dragged into a secret and she wasn't willing to keep it quiet, not to Isaac. "Sorry, *Mamm*, but he'll have to know. We're going to be married and I want him to know about my half-*bruder*."

Mamm nodded. "Only tell him, then, and ask him to keep it quiet. I hope this isn't going to be spread around now. Shame will come upon us if it does."

"We won't tell anyone, *Mamm*," Favor said.

When they heard a buggy, Joy jumped up and raced to the window. "It's Isaac and I haven't even started dinner."

"I'm going to see Carter now," Florence rose to her feet.

"Are you going to tell him everything?" Wilma asked.

"I am. I don't see the point of delaying it."

"It's dark out."

"I'll take a flashlight." Florence hurried away and took hold of the flashlight by the back door. Everything made sense now. That explained why Wilma's stories about Iris had varied. That was why *Mamm* was so upset about her reading that letter from Gerald and why she tossed it into the flames of their open fire. New lies had covered old ones until the burden of the lies became too much. She wondered, though, if Wilma would have carried these secrets and lies to her grave if Carter hadn't come to live in the Bakers' former guest cottage. Would her stepmother ever have told 'her girls' that they had a half-brother out there somewhere?

As Florence made her way through the darkness of the orchard, she hoped Carter wouldn't be too distraught when he learned Iris wasn't his birthmother. If only she wasn't the one who had to tell him this news. Once again, Wilma had laid her own responsibility on Florence's shoulders.

Losing the orchard didn't seem so important now. Carter was what mattered.

CHAPTER 22

SHE WAS RELIEVED when she saw smoke coming out of the chimney and a golden light coming from his window. He was home and she could get this news off her chest.

He opened the door as though he had known she was coming. "Florence! How long have you been back?"

"Only a couple of hours."

A black and white dog bounded toward her, barking.

He looked down at the dog. "Meet Spot."

She crouched down and patted him. "Hello, Spot." The dog sniffed her and then licked her face.

"He likes you."

She stood up and Carter hugged her. "You said you'd call as soon as you got home."

"I'm home now. Whenever I'm in your arms, I'm home."

"That's exactly how I feel." He stepped back a little when she started sobbing. "What's wrong?"

"Everything." She stepped forward and cried on his shoulder as all the stress of the last few days came to the surface.

"Come inside." He carefully moved her through to the couch. "What's upset you? I'm sure the funeral and all that wouldn't have been pleasant."

"I wanted *Mamm* to tell the girls you're their cousin, but instead she said …" She couldn't even say the words.

He held her hand. "Go on."

"Instead, she said she's getting married, and I'm not welcome there anymore. Her husband is going to run the orchard, and he knows nothing."

"I'm sorry, Florence, but didn't we expect this might happen?"

"I *thought* it might, but I didn't *expect* it to. And, there's more."

"What? Tell me."

She sniffed, and now she was more concerned about him than herself. "She told the girls the truth about you and Iris, but it wasn't what we expected. She had a different story to tell."

He tilted his head to the side. "What did she say?"

She touched his arm. "What do you know about your birth mother?"

He frowned. "Just tell me what she said. You won't upset me."

"She said she was your mother and not Iris."

He didn't look surprised. Slowly, he nodded.

"Is it the truth?" she asked.

"I'm sorry to have kept you in the dark, Florence, but it wasn't my place to say anything. I thought Iris was my mother and then when my father died, she told me everything. But, she made me promise I'd never go looking for Wilma. She said Wilma would upset me because she'd want nothing to do with me. Seems she was right."

"I can't believe you knew."

"I'm sorry. Do you forgive me?"

"I do. Yes, totally. And I'm pleased the news isn't coming as a shock to you."

"I had hoped Wilma would admit to it the other day when we told her Iris had died, but she didn't. Then I thought she was going to keep her secret to the grave."

"She told my father she'd had a child, but he never said anything to any of us. I don't think he said anything to Earl or Mark, either. If he did, they didn't say." She felt all tension leave her. When she was with him, nothing else mattered.

"Now we've both been rejected by Wilma."

"That's right."

"It looks like you've lost your orchard."

"She said it's all hers and I'm not welcome, and she's getting married and I have to leave."

"Ah, I'm sorry about that."

"Me too."

"I have the solution. I bought up the next three properties moving that way." He pointed to the opposite side of where her orchard was.

She stared at him. He'd mentioned it so casually, like he'd just gone out and bought an ice-cream. "They sold to you?"

"I can be persuasive when I want to be. I have been working on it for a while and now they're ours."

"Already?"

He nodded. "It was a surprise, but now you know. It'll take some years to establish the soil and the plants to the level where you can get organic accreditation, but … apart from getting married and raising a family, what else would we do?"

She laughed. "I can't believe you."

"Do you trust me?"

"I do."

"I'll help you with the orchard. It's a project we can do together. If you want my help that is. If not, I'll be able to keep myself busy with plenty of other things."

"I'd love it if we did it together. Did it as a family."

He smiled. "I like the sound of that. Come away with me tomorrow and we'll get married. No, forget that. Come with me now. I'm through with waiting. If you go back there, something will happen, someone will make you feel guilty, or you'll change your mind and you'll keep putting this off."

She giggled, wanting to do as he suggested and throw caution to the wind.

"I'm serious, Florence, I love you more than life itself."

"This sounds crazy, but I will. Yes, I will. I'll have to go back and get my things."

"No." He shook his head and handed her his cell phone. "Call them. Tell them we're eloping and you'll come see them when you get back from your ... our honeymoon."

She gulped and took hold of his phone. "But there are so many things that need to be organized. There are things that only I know how to do."

"What better way for them to learn?"

"Spot. Who will look after him?"

"I'll take him to Maggie's place. She's a free woman now, did I tell you?"

"No, you didn't."

"She's looking for a new home for Spot. She's moving to an apartment. Here, he can run around on all this land. What do you say?"

She looked down at Spot. "We can keep him?"

He nodded. "I kind of already told her I'd have him."

"That's wonderful!"

"Really? You don't mind?"

"Not at all."

"Good. She won't mind looking after him for a few days and we'll collect him on our way back."

"He's the first member of our family."

"He is. Of our large family that we hope to have."

She smiled loving the fact that they wanted the same things out of life. Looking down at the phone in her hands, she said, "I don't know how this works." He took it from her, pressed a few buttons and handed it back to her.

"That's the number you gave me."

Florence's heart beat fast as the phone beeped. Then Cherish answered. "Cherish. It's Florence."

"Florence?"

"*Jah.* I've called to tell you something and you can pass it on to everyone."

"Where are you?"

"I'm next door at Carter's place. I'm eloping with him. We're getting married and I'm never coming back to the *haus.* I'll say goodbye to you all when I get back from my honeymoon." When there was silence, Florence asked, "Are you still there?"

"*Jah.* I'm just thinking up what I'll say to *Mamm.*"

"Tell her the truth."

"The truth? Are you sure?"

Florence giggled. "Yes. There have been too many lies. I'm an adult and I'm leaving to marry Carter."

"Good for you. I can't wait until I'm an adult. You *will* bring him back to meet us, won't you?"

"For certain. You might have to come to our place, but either way, I promise you'll get to meet your half-brother. I'll make certain of it."

"You're the best *schweschder* ever, Florence."

"Good night, Cherish. I'll miss you all."

"The place won't be the same without you, but you're doing the right thing. I want to be you when I grow up." Cherish giggled again. "Good night, Florence."

"Night." Florence didn't know how to end a call so she handed the phone back to Carter. He pressed the end button and tossed the phone onto the couch.

He stretched out his arms and she stood up and he pulled her toward him and their lips met. "Let's go, Mrs. Braithwaite."

"I'm not Mrs. Braithwaite yet."

He glanced at his watch. "It's literally only a matter of time."

It didn't take them long for Florence to exchange her Amish clothes for a dress and cardigan. Then she removed her prayer kapp and let her hair fall down. She knew she'd have to cut it soon. Unless her hair was up all the time it was going to get in the way. Next they packed their bags, took Spot to Maggie's house, and then they sped off into the night heading for Florida where they could marry without delay.

Florence prayed her family wouldn't turn their backs on her. There was Mercy's baby to cuddle when it arrived, there was Joy and Isaac's wedding coming later in the year, and she wanted to know how Cherish would get on with her farm and whether her caretaker would do a good job. Would Wilma really go through with marrying Levi? Would she and Carter be invited? And if Wilma and Levi married, would he ruin all the hard work her father and she had put into the orchard?

Whatever her future held, she knew God had His hands on her and on Carter.

She was leaving her family and her orchard behind for new beginnings that would be surrounded by love, many children, and of course, apple trees.

THE AMISH BONNET SISTERS

Book 1 Amish Mercy

Book 2 Amish Honor

Book 3 A Simple Kiss

Book 4 Amish Joy

Book 5 Amish Family Secrets

Book 6 The Englisher

Book 7 Missing Florence

Book 8 Their Amish Stepfather

Book 9 A Baby For Florence.

ABOUT SAMANTHA PRICE

USA Today Bestselling author, Samantha Price, wrote stories from a young age, but it wasn't until later in life that she took up writing full time. Formally an artist, she exchanged her paintbrush for the computer and, many best-selling book series later, has never looked back.

Samantha is happiest on her computer lost in the world of her characters. She is best known for the Ettie Smith Amish Mysteries series and the Expectant Amish Widows series.

www.SamanthaPriceAuthor.com

Samantha loves to hear from her readers. Connect with her at:

samantha@samanthapriceauthor.com

www.facebook.com/SamanthaPriceAuthor

Follow Samantha Price on BookBub

Twitter @ AmishRomance

Instagram - SamanthaPriceAuthor

Made in the USA
Coppell, TX
12 December 2021